'Yo

Dan shifted his
across at her
course this

Emma simply looked back at him, her brown eyes
serious.

'Well, technically, no,' she said. 'Because we'd have
to be in a *proper* relationship for me to do that, and
ours is a fake one.' She put her head on one side. 'If
it's actually one at all. To be honest, it's more of an
arrangement, isn't it? A plus-one agreement.'

He'd never been dumped before. It was an odd
novelty. And certainly not by a real girlfriend. It
seemed being dumped by a fake one was no less of a
shock to the system.

'It's been good while it lasted,' she was saying.
'Mutually beneficial for both of us. You got a
professional plus-one for your work engagements
and I got my parents off my back. But the fact is—'

'It's not you, it's me?' he joked, still not convinced
she wasn't messing around.

5

... is my fourth book. ... for this fabulously ...eries, and I'm still pinching my... ...ake sure I'm not dreaming!

Talking of flirty... We've all had times when the dating game seems more trouble than it's worth—I know I have. In that kind of situation wouldn't it be great if you had a person on the end of the phone who could fit the bill as your date, no matter what the occasion? Someone who would always step up to the plate, make the right impression and never let you down or show you up? Wouldn't that make life easier?

Just as long as you don't fall in love with your perfect platonic plus-one, of course. Imagine the mayhem *that* could cause. Especially at a big family occasion where good impressions really count.

I've had so much fun playing around with these ideas while writing this story, and I hope you will have a lovely time reading it too.

Love

Charlotte x

THE PLUS-ONE AGREEMENT

BY
CHARLOTTE PHILLIPS

MILLS & BOON

Published in Great Britain 2014
by Mills & Boon, an imprint of Harlequin (UK) Limited,
Eton House, 18-24 Paradise Road, Richmond, Surrey, TW9 1SR

© 2014 Charlotte Phillips

ISBN: 978 0 263 91087 2

Harlequin (UK) Limited's policy is to use papers that are natural,
renewable and recyclable products and made from wood grown in
sustainable forests. The logging and manufacturing processes conform
to the legal environmental regulations of the country of origin.

Printed and bound in Spain
by Blackprint CPI, Barcelona

Charlotte Phillips has been reading romantic fiction since her teens, and she adores upbeat stories with happy endings. Writing them for Mills & Boon is her dream job. She combines writing with looking after her fabulous husband, two teenagers, a four-year-old and a dachshund. When something has to give, it's usually housework. She lives in Wiltshire.

**This and other books by Charlotte Phillips
are available in eBook format
from www.millsandboon.co.uk**

For Gemma, who makes my day every day.
With all my love always.

CHAPTER ONE

Q: How do you tell your fake boyfriend that you've met a real one and you don't need him any more?

A: However you like. If he's not a real boyfriend, it's not a real break-up. Hardly likely that he'll start declaring undying love for you, is it?

CHANCE WOULD HAVE been a fine thing.

This Aston Martin might fly before arm candy addict Dan Morgan developed anything more than a fake attraction for someone as sensible and boring as Emma Burney, and it wasn't as if she hadn't given it time. Getting on for a year in his company, watching an endless string of short-term flings pout their way through his private life, had convinced her she was never going to be blonde enough, curvy enough or vacuous enough to qualify. In fact she was pretty much the opposite of all his conquests, even dressed up to the nines for her brother's art exhibition.

She glanced down at herself in the plain black boatneck frock and nude heels she'd chosen, teamed as usual with her minimal make-up and straight-up-and-down figure. Romance need not apply.

She did, however, possess all the qualities Dan wanted in a supportive friend and social ally. As he did for her. Hence the fake part of their agreement.

An agreement which she reminded herself she no longer needed.

Not if she wanted to move forward from the suspended animation that had been her life this last year. Any residual hope that what was counterfeit between them might somehow turn genuine if she just gave it enough time had been squashed in these last few amazing weeks as she'd been swept off her feet by a whirlwind of intimate, luxurious dinners, expensive gifts and exciting plans. What was between her and Dan was now nothing more than a rut that needed climbing out of.

She watched him quietly for a moment from the passenger seat of his car, looking like an aftershave model in his dark suit and white shirt. His dark hair was so thick there was always a hint of spike about it, a light shadow of stubble lined his jaw, and his ice-blue eyes and slow smile had the ability to charm the entire female species. It had certainly worked on her mother, whose ongoing mission in life was to get Emma and Dan married off and raising a tribe of kids like some Fifties cupcake couple.

Perpetuating her gene pool was the last thing Emma wanted—a lifetime in the midst of her insane family had seen to that. Having Dan as her pretend boyfriend at family events had proved to be the perfect fob-off.

But now she had the real thing and the pretending was holding her back. All that remained was to explain that fact to Dan. She gathered herself together and took a deep breath.

'This has to stop,' she said.

* * *

'You're dumping me?'

Dan shifted his eyes briefly from the road to glance across at her, a mock grin on his face. Because of course this was some kind of joke, right? She simply looked back at him, her brown eyes serious.

'Well, technically, no,' she said. 'Because we'd have to be in a *proper* relationship for me to do that, and ours is a fake one.' She put her head on one side. 'If it's actually one at all. To be honest, it's more of an agreement, isn't it? A plus-one agreement.'

He'd never seen fit to give it a name before. It had simply been an extension of their work dealings into a mutually beneficial social arrangement. There had been no conscious decision or drawing up of terms. It had just grown organically from one simple work success.

Twelve months ago Emma, in her capacity as his lawyer, had attended a meeting with Dan and a potential client for his management consultancy. A potentially huge client. The meeting had overrun into dinner, she had proved a formidable ally and his winning of the contract had been smoothed along perfectly by their double act. She had seemed to bounce off him effortlessly, predicting where he was taking the conversation, backing him up where he needed it. He'd ended the evening with a new client, a new respect for Emma and the beginnings of a connection.

After that she'd become his go-to ally for social engagements—a purely platonic date that he could count on for intelligent conversation and professional behaviour. She'd become a trusted contact. And in return he'd accompanied her to family dinners and events like this one today, sympathising with her exasperation at her slightly crazy family while not really understanding it.

Surely better to have a slightly crazy family than no family at all?

He'd never been dumped before. It was an odd novelty. And certainly not by a real girlfriend. It seemed being dumped by a fake one was no less of a shock to the system.

'It's been good while it lasted,' she was saying. 'Mutually beneficial for both of us. You got a professional plus-one for your work engagements and I got my parents off my back. But the fact is—'

'It's not you, it's me?' he joked, still not convinced she wasn't messing around.

'I've met someone,' she said, not smiling.

'Someone?' he said, shaking his head lightly and reaching for the air-conditioning controls. For some reason it was suddenly boiling in the car. 'A work someone?'

'No, not a work someone!' Her tone was exasperated. 'Despite what you might think, I do have a life, you know—outside work.'

'I never said you didn't.'

He glanced across at her indignant expression just as it melted into a smile of triumph.

'Dan, I've *met* someone.'

She held his gaze for a second before he looked back at the road, her eyebrows slightly raised, waiting for him to catch on. He tried to keep a grin in place when for some reason his face wanted to fold in on itself. In the months he'd known her she'd been on maybe two or three dates, to his knowledge, and none of the men involved had ever been important enough to her to earn the description 'someone'.

He sat back in his seat and concentrated hard on driving the car through the London evening traffic. He supposed she was waiting for some kind of congratulatory comment and he groped for one.

'Good for you,' he said eventually. 'Who is he?'

'He was involved in some legal work I was doing.'

So she *had* met him through her job as a lawyer, then. Of course she had. When did she ever do anything that wasn't somehow linked to work? Even their own friendship was based in work. It had started with work and had grown with their mutual ambition.

'We've been on a few dates and it's going really well.' She took a breath. 'And that's why I need to end things with you.'

Things? For some reason he disliked the vagueness of the term, as if it meant nothing.

'You don't date,' he pointed out.

'Exactly,' she said, jabbing a finger at him. 'And do you know *why* I don't date?'

'Because no man could possibly match up to me?'

'Despite what you might think is appealing to women, I don't relish the prospect of a couple of nights sharing your bed only to be kicked out of it the moment you get bored.'

'No need to make it sound so brutal. They all go into it with their eyes open, you know. I don't make any false promises that it will ever be more than a bit of fun.'

'None of them ever believe that. They all think they'll be the one to change you. But you'll never change because you don't need to. You've got me for the times when you need to be serious, so you can keep the rest of your girlies just for fun.'

She looked down at her hands, folded in her lap.

'The thing is, Dan, passing you off as my boyfriend

might keep my family off my back, and it stops the swipes about me being single and the comments about my biological clock, but it doesn't actually solve anything. I didn't realise until now that I'm in a rut. I haven't dated for months. All I do is work. It's so easy to rely on you if I have to go anywhere I need a date that I've quit looking for anyone else.'

'What are you saying?'

She sighed.

'Just that meeting Alistair has opened my eyes to what I've been missing. And I really think our agreement is holding us both back.'

'Alistair?'

'His name is Alistair Woods.'

He easily dismissed the image that zipped into his brain of the blond ex-international cycling star, because it had to be a coincidence. Emma didn't know anyone like *that*. He would know if she did. Except she was waiting, lips slightly parted, eyebrows slightly raised. Everything about her expression told him she was waiting for him to catch on.

'Not *the* Alistair Woods?' he said, because she so obviously wanted him to.

He stole a glance across at her and the smile that lit up her face caused a sorry twist somewhere deep in his stomach. It was a smile he couldn't remember seeing for the longest time—not since they'd first met.

The glance turned into a look for as long as safe driving would allow, during which he saw her with an unusually objective eye, noticing details that had passed him by before. The hint of colour touching the smooth high cheekbones, the soft fullness of her lower lip, the way tendrils of her dark hair curled softly against the creamy skin of her shoulders in the boat-neck dress. She looked absolutely radiant and his stomach gave a slow and unmistakable flip, adding to his sense of unreality.

'Exactly,' she said with a touch of triumph. 'The cyclist. Well, ex-cyclist. He's in TV now—he does presenting and commentating.'

Of course he did. His face had been a permanent media fixture during the last big sports event in the UK. Dan felt a sudden irrational aversion to the man, whom he'd never met.

'*You're* dating Alistair Woods?'

He failed to keep the incredulity out of his voice and it earned him a flash of anger that replaced her bubbling excitement like a flood of cold water.

'No need to make it sound so unbelievable,' she snapped. 'You might only see me as some power suit, great for taking on the difficult dates when one of your five-minute conquests won't make the right impression, but I do actually have a dual existence. As a woman.'

'How long have you been seeing him?' he said.

'What are you? My father?' she said. 'We've been out a few times.'

'How many is a few?'

'Half a dozen, maybe.'

'You're ending our agreement on the strength of half a dozen dates?'

'Yes, well, they weren't dates in the way you think of them. He hasn't just invited me out for an impressive dinner as a preamble to taking me to bed. You can actually get to know someone really well in half a dozen dates if you approach them in a more…*serious* way.'

The thinly veiled dig didn't escape him and indignation sharpened his voice.

'OK, then, if he's so bloody marvellous, and you're so bloody smitten, why the hell isn't *he* on his way to look at your brother's wacky paintings and meet the parents? Couldn't you have dumped me on the phone and saved me a load of time and hassle?'

He pulled the car to a standstill outside the gallery steps and turned off the engine.

'I'm not dumping you! How many times? It's a *fake* relationship!'

A uniformed attendant opened Emma's car door and she got out. Dan threw his keys to the parking valet and joined her on the steps.

'So you keep saying,' he said, keeping his voice low. 'I could have spent this evening working.'

'Like you don't spend enough of your life doing that.' She led the way through the high arched doorway into the gallery. 'You can easily afford an evening. Alistair's out of the country until next week, and I need this opportunity to draw a thick, black and irreversible line under the two of us for my parents' eyes and undo the tissue of fibs I've told them.'

They walked slowly down the red-carpeted hallway, his hand pressed softly at the small of her back—the perfect escort as always.

'I really don't see why I need to be there for you to do that,' he said, smiling politely at other guests as they passed, maintaining the perfect impression. 'Especially since it's only a *fake* relationship.'

Even as he piled heavy sarcasm on the word *fake* he wondered why the hell he was turning this into such a big deal. Why should he care? It had simply been a handy arrangement, nothing more.

'Because the problem with it being a fake relationship

is that it was a pretty damn perfect one,' she snapped. 'And so now I need a fake break-up.'

She outlined her suggestion as they walked down the hall and it sounded so insane that his mind had trouble processing it.

'You can't possibly be serious. You want to fake an argument in front of your family so you can make some kind of a righteous point by dumping me?'

'Exactly! Shouldn't be too hard. I'll choose a moment, start picking on you, and then you just play along.'

'Why can't you just tell them we broke up? That things didn't work out?' He ran an exasperated hand through his hair. 'Why do I need to be here at all?'

'Because I've spent the last year building you up as Mr Perfect, bigging you up at every opportunity. You've no idea what it was like before we started helping each other out. The constant questions about why I was still single, the hassle about my body clock careering towards a standstill, the negativity about my career. Introducing you as my boyfriend stopped all that like magic. They think you're the son-in-law of their dreams—a rich businessman who adores me, good-looking, charming, not remotely fazed by my mother. They'll never just take my word for it that we broke up amicably. I'd spend the rest of my days being questioned about what I did to drive you away. You'd be forever name-dropped as the one that got away. No man I bring home would ever live up to your perfect memory.'

'You don't think you're going a bit overboard?'

'Are you really asking me that? You've met my mother. You know what she's like.'

He had to concede that Emma's mother was without a doubt the most interfering person he'd ever come across, with an opinion about everything that was never wrong. Her relationship with Emma seemed to bring out the critic in both of them. Mutual exasperated affection was probably the nearest he could get to describing it.

'This way your fabulous reputation will be ruined, by the time Alistair and I finish our trip to the States you'll be a distant memory, and they'll be ready to accept him as my new man.' She shrugged. 'Once I've…you know… *briefed* him on what they can be like.'

Trip to the States? His hands felt clammy. He stopped outside the main gallery and pulled her to one side before they could get swept into the room by the crowd.

'You're going on holiday?'

She looked at him impatiently.

'In a few weeks' time, yes. I'm going to meet some of his friends and family. And then after that I'm going to travel with him in Europe while he covers an international cycling race for American TV. I'm taking a sabbatical from work. I might not even come back.'

'What?' His mind reeled. 'You're giving up your life as you know it on the strength of a few dates? Are you mad?'

'That's exactly it! When do I *ever* do anything impetuous? It isn't as if sensible planning has worked out so well for me, is it? I work all hours and I have no social life to speak of beyond filling in for you. What exactly have I got to lose?'

'What about your family?'

'I'm hardly going to be missed, am I? My parents are so busy following Adam's ascent to celebrity status with his art that they're not going to start showing an interest in my life.'

She leaned in towards him and lowered her voice, treating him to the dizzying scent of her vanilla perfume.

'One of his pictures went for five figures last month, you know. Some anonymous buyer, apparently. But two words about *my* work and they start to glaze over.'

She leaned back again and took a small mirror from her clutch bag.

'And you'll be fine, of course,' she went on, opening the mirror and checking her face in it, oblivious to his floundering brain. 'You must have a whole little black book of girls who'd fall over themselves to step into my shoes. You're hardly going to be stuck for a date.'

True enough. He might, however, be stuck for a date who made the right kind of impression. Wasn't that how this whole agreement of theirs had started? He didn't go in for dating with a serious slant—not any more. Not since Maggie and…

He clenched his fists. Even after all these years thoughts of her and their failed plans occasionally filtered into his mind, despite the effort he put into forgetting them. There was no place for those memories in his life. These days for him it was all about keeping full control. Easy fun, then moving on. Unfortunately the girls who fitted that kind of mould didn't have the right fit in work circles. Emma had filled that void neatly, meaning he could bed whoever the hell he liked because he had her for the serious stuff—the stuff where impressions counted.

It occurred to him for the first time that she wouldn't just be across London if he needed her. He felt oddly unsettled as she tugged at his arm and walked towards the main door.

'You've had some mad ideas in your time, but this…' he said.

* * *

As they entered the main gallery Emma paused to take in the enormity of what her brother had achieved. The vast room had a spectacular landing running above it, from which the buzzing exhibition could be viewed. It had been divided into groupings by display screens, on which Adam's paintings—some of them taller than her—were picked out in pools of perfect clear lighting. A crowd of murmuring spectators surrounded the nearest one, which depicted an enormous eyeball with tiny cavorting people in the centre of it. His work might not be her cup of tea, but it certainly commanded attention and evoked strong opinions. Just the way he always had done.

She took two crystal flutes of champagne from the silver tray of a pretty blonde attendant, who looked straight through her to smile warmly at Dan. For heaven's sake, was no woman immune? Emma handed him one of the flutes and he immediately raised it to the blonde girl.

'Thanks very much…' He leaned in close so he could read the name tag conveniently pinned next to a cleavage Emma could only ever dream of owning. 'Hannah…'

He returned the girl's smile. Emma dragged him away. Why was she even surprised? Didn't she know him well enough by now? No woman was safe.

Correction: no curvy blonde arm candy was safe.

'For Pete's sake, pay attention,' she said in a stage whisper. 'You're meant to be here with me, not eyeing up the staff.'

She linked her arm through his so she could propel him through the crowd to find her parents. It wasn't difficult. Her mother had for some insane reason chosen to wear a wide flowing scarf wrapped around her head and tied to one side. Emma headed through the crowd, aiming for it—aqua silk with a feather pin stuck in it on one side. As her parents fell into possible earshot she pasted on a smile and talked through her beaming teeth.

'They'll never just take my word for it that we've just gone our separate ways. Not without a massive inquest. And I can't be doing with that. Trust me, it'll work better this way. It's cleaner. Just go with everything I say.'

She speeded up the end of the sentence as her mother approached.

'And you don't need to worry,' she added from the corner of her mouth. 'I'll pay for the dry-cleaning.'

'You'll what? What the hell is *that* supposed to mean?'

He turned his face towards her, a puzzled frown lightly creasing his forehead, and his eyes followed her hand as she raised her flute of champagne, ready to tip the contents over his head. She saw his blue eyes widen in sudden understanding and realised far too late that she'd totally underestimated his reflexes.

Dan's hand shot out instantly to divert hers, knocking it to one side in a single lightning movement. And instead of providing the explosive beginning to her staged *we're finished* argument, the glass jerked sharply sideways and emptied itself in a huge splash down the front of her mother's aquamarine jumpsuit. She stared in horror as champagne soaked into the fabric, lending it a translucent quality that revealed an undergarment not unlike a parachute harness.

She'd inadvertently turned her mother into Miss Wet T-Shirt, London. And if she'd been a disappointing daughter before, this bumped things up to a whole new level.

CHAPTER TWO

'Aaaaargh!'

The ensuing squawk from Emma's mother easily outdid the gallery's classy background music, and Dan was dimly aware of the room falling silent around them as people turned from the paintings to watch.

'An accident—it was an accident...' Emma gabbled, fumbling with a pack of tissues from her tiny clutch bag and making a futile attempt at mopping up the mess.

As her father shook a handkerchief from his pocket and joined in, her mother slapped his hand away in exasperation.

'It'll take more than a few tissues,' she snarled furiously at him, and then turned on Emma. 'Do you know how much this outfit *cost*? How am I meant to stand next to your brother in the publicity photos now? I've never known anyone so *clumsy.*'

Emma's face was the colour of beetroot, but any sympathy Dan might have felt was rather undermined by the revelation that she'd intended, without so much as a word of warning, to make a fool of him in front of the cream of London's social scene. *That* was her plan? *That?* Dumping him publicly by humiliating him? If he hadn't caught on in time it would have been him standing there dripping Veuve Clicquot while she no doubt laid into him with a ludicrous fake argument.

No one dumped him. *Ever.*

'An accident?' he said pointedly.

She glanced towards him, her red face one enormous fluster. He raised furious eyebrows and mouthed the word *dry-cleaning* at her. She widened her eyes back at him in an apologetic please-stick-to-the-plan gesture.

Emma's brother, Adam, pushed his way through the crowd, turning perfectly coiffed heads as he went, dandyish as ever in a plum velvet jacket with a frothy lace shirt underneath. There was concern in his eyes behind his statement glasses.

'What's going on, people?' he said, staring in surprise at his mother as she shrugged her way into her husband's jacket and fastened the buttons grimly to hide the stain.

'Your sister has just flung champagne *all over me,*' she snapped dramatically, then raised both hands as Adam opened his mouth to speak. 'No, no, don't you go worrying about it, I'm not going anywhere. I wouldn't *hear* of it. This is your night. I'm not going to let the fact that my outfit is *decimated* ruin that. I'll soldier on, just like I always do.'

'I've said I'm sorry. I'll pay for the dry-cleaning,' Emma said desperately.

Dan's anger slipped a notch as he picked up on her discomfort. Only a notch, mind you. OK, so maybe he wouldn't have it out with her in public, but he would most certainly be dealing with her later.

Emma closed her eyes briefly. When did it end? Would everything she ever did in life, good or bad, be somehow referenced by Adam's success? Then again, since her mother was already furious with her, she might

as well press ahead with the planned mock break-up.
Maybe then at least the evening wouldn't be a total
write-off.

She drew Dan aside by the elbow as Adam drifted
away again, back to his adoring public.

'We can still do it,' she said. 'We can still stage the
break-up.'

He stared at her incredulously.

'Are you having some kind of a laugh?' he snapped.
'When you said you needed a fake break-up I wasn't expecting it to involve my public humiliation. You were
going to lob that drink over *me,* for heaven's sake, and
now you think I'll just agree to a rerun?'

She opened her mouth to respond and he cut her off.

'There are people I *know* in here,' he said in a furious stage whisper, nodding around them at the crowd.
'What kind of impression do you think that would have
given them?'

'I didn't expect things to get so out of hand,' she said.
'I just thought we'd have a quick mock row in front of
my parents and that would be it.'

'You didn't even warn me!'

'I didn't want to lose the element of surprise. I wanted
to make it look, you know, *authentic.*'

He stared at her in disbelief.

There was the squeal of whiny microphone feedback
and Adam appeared on the landing above the gallery.
Emma looked up towards her brother, picked out in a
pool of light in front of a billboard with his own name on
it in six-foot-tall violet letters. She felt overshadowed, as
always, by his brilliance. Just as she had done at school.
But now it was on a much more glamorous level. No
wonder her legal career seemed drab in comparison.

No wonder her parents were expecting her to give it all up at any moment to get married and give them grand-children. Adam was far too good for such normal, boring life plans.

His voice began to boom over the audio system, thanking everyone for coming and crediting a list of people she'd never heard of with his success.

'I can't believe you'd make a scene like that without considering what effect it might have on me,' Dan said, anger still lacing his voice.

The blonde champagne waitress chose that moment to walk past them. Emma watched as Dan's gaze flickered away from her to follow the woman's progress and the grovelling apology she'd been about to give screeched to a halt on the tip of her tongue. Just who the hell did he think he was, moaning about being dumped, when *his* relationship principles were pretty much in the gutter? OK, so they might not have actually *been* a couple, but she'd seen the trail of broken hearts he left in his wake. He had no relationship scruples whatsoever. One girl followed another. And as soon as he'd got what he wanted he lost interest and dumped them. As far as she knew he'd never suffered a moment's comeback as a result.

Maybe this new improved Emma, with her stupid unrequited girlie crush on Dan well and truly in the past, had a duty to press that point on behalf of womankind.

'Oh, get over yourself,' she said, before she could change her mind. 'I'd say a public dumping was probably long overdue. It's just that none of your conquests have had the nous or the self-respect to do it before. There's probably a harem of curvy blonde waitresses and models who've thought about lobbing a drink over you when you've chucked them just because you're bored.

And I didn't actually spill a drop on you, so let's just move on, shall we?'

Adam smiled and laughed his way back through the crowd towards them, and she seized the opportunity as he neared her proudly beaming parents.

'Same plan as before, minus the champagne. I'll start picking on you and…'

The words trailed away in her mouth as Adam clamped one arm around Dan's shoulders and one around her own.

'Got some news for you all—gather round, gather round,' he said.

As her parents moved in closer, questioning expressions on their faces, he raised both hands in a gesture of triumph above his head.

'Be happy for me, people!'

He performed a jokey pirouette and finished with a manic grin and jazz hands.

'Ernie and I are getting married!'

Beaming at them, he slid his velvet-sleeved arm around his boyfriend and pulled him into a hot kiss.

Her mother's gasp of shock was audible above the cheers. And any plans Emma might have had of staging a limelight-stealing break-up went straight back to the drawing board.

Emma watched the buzzing crowd of people now surrounding Adam and Ernie, showering them with congratulations, vaguely relieved that she hadn't managed to dispense with Dan after all. From the tense look on her parents' faces, as they stood well away from the throng, dealing with the fallout from Adam's announcement wasn't going to be easy. And despite the fact that it was a setback in her plans to introduce Alistair, there was no doubt that her mother was much easier to handle when she had Dan in her corner.

Dealing with her parents without him was something she hadn't had to do in so long that she hadn't realised how she'd come to rely on his calming presence. They might have only been helping each other out, but Dan had had her back where her family were concerned. And he'd never been remotely fazed by her overbearing mother and downtrodden father.

She wondered for the first time with a spike of doubt whether Alistair would be as supportive as that. Or would he let her family cloud his judgement of her? What was that saying? *Look at the mother if you want to see your future wife.* If that theory held up she might as well join a nunnery. Alistair would be out of her life before she could blink.

She couldn't let herself think like that.

Calling a halt with Dan was clearly the right thing to do if she was so ridiculously dependent on him that she could no longer handle her family on her own. But she couldn't ruin Adam's excitement. Not tonight. She'd simply have to reschedule things.

And in the meantime at least she wasn't handling her mother's shock by herself. She took a new flute of champagne gratefully from Dan and braced herself with a big sip.

'I'm sure it must just be a publicity stunt,' her mother was saying.

Denial. Her mother's stock reaction to news she didn't want to hear.

'It's not a publicity stunt,' Adam said. 'We're getting married.'

He beamed at Ernie, standing beside him in a slim-cut electric blue suit. He certainly *looked* the perfect match for Adam.

Her mother's jaw didn't even really drop. Disbelief was so ingrained in her.

'Don't be ridiculous, darling,' she said, flicking an invisible speck of dirt from Adam's lapel. 'Of course you're not.'

Adam's face took on the stoic expression of one who knew he would need to press the point more than once in order to be heard. Possibly a few hundred times.

'It's the next logical step,' he said.

'In what?' Her mother flapped a dismissive hand. 'It's just a phase. You'll soon snap out of it once the right girl comes along. Bit like Emma with her vegetarian thing back in the day.' She nodded at Emma. 'Soon went back to normal after a couple of weeks when she fancied a bacon sandwich.'

'Mum,' Adam said patiently, 'Emma was thirteen. I'm twenty-nine. Ernie and I have been together for nearly a year.'

'I know. Sharing a flat. Couple of lads. No need to turn it into more than it is.'

Emma stared as Adam finally raised his voice enough to make her mother stop talking.

'Mum, you're in denial!'

As she stopped her protests and looked at him he took a deep breath and lowered his voice, speaking with the tired patience of someone who'd covered the same ground many times, only to end up where he'd started.

'I've been out since I was eighteen. I know you've never wanted to accept it, but the right girl for me *doesn't exist*. We're having a civil partnership ceremony in six weeks' time and I want you all to be there and be happy for me.'

'I'm happy for you,' Emma said, smiling tentatively.

Happiness she could do. Unfortunately being at the wedding might be a bit trickier. Her plans with Alistair lurked at the edge of her mind. She'd been so excited about going away with him. He'd showered her with gifts and attention, and for the first time in her life she was being blown away by being the sole focus of another person. And not just any person. Alistair Woods had to be one of the most eligible bachelors in the universe, with an army of female fans, and he had chosen to be with *her*. She still couldn't quite believe her luck. Their trip was planned to the hilt. She would have to make Adam understand somehow.

He leaned in and gave her a hug. 'Thanks, Em.'

She had grown up feeling overshadowed by Adam's achievements. Just the look of him was attention-grabbing, with his perfectly chiselled features and foppish dress sense. And that was just now. She couldn't forget the school years, where for every one of Emma's hard-earned A grades there had been a matching two or three showered effortlessly on Adam. His flamboyant, outgoing personality charmed everyone he came into contact with, and her mother never ceased championing his successes to anyone who would listen.

It hadn't been easy being her parents' Plan B. Competing for their interest with someone as dazzling as Adam was an impossible, cold task.

'I blame you for this, Donald,' her mother snapped at her father. 'Indulging his ridiculous obsession with musical theatre when he was in his teens.'

Sometimes Emma forgot that being her parents' Plan A was probably no picnic either.

Adam held up his hands.

'Please, Mum. It's not up for discussion. It's happening with or without your approval. Can't you just be pleased for us?'

There was an extremely long pause and then her mother gave an enormous grudging sigh.

'Well, I can kiss goodbye to grandchildren, I suppose,' she grumbled. 'We'll have to count on you for that now, Emma. *If* you can ever manage to find a man who'll commit.'

She glared pointedly at Dan, who totally ignored the jibe. Emma had been wondering how long it would be before her biological clock got a mention. Terrific. So now Adam could carve out the life he wanted without bearing the brunt of her parents' wrath because they had Emma lined up as their biological backup plan to carry on their insane gene pool.

Going away with Alistair was beginning to feel like a lucky escape. She just needed to get her plans back on track.

Dan scanned an e-mail for the third time and realised he still hadn't properly taken it in. His mind had been all over the place this last day or two.

Since the night of Adam's exhibition, to be exact.

There was a gnawing feeling deep in his gut that work didn't seem to be suppressing, and he finally threw in the towel on distracting himself, took his mind off work and applied it to the problem instead.

He was piqued because Emma had ended things with him. OK, so her plans to dump him publicly hadn't come off, thankfully, but the end result was the same. She'd drawn a line under their relationship without so much as a moment's pause and he hadn't heard from her since. No discussion, no input from him.

He was even more piqued because now it was over with he really shouldn't give a damn. They were friends, work colleagues, and that was all there was to it. Their romantic attachment existed only in the impression they'd given to the outside world, to work contacts and her family. It had always been a front.

His pique had absolutely nothing to do with any sudden realisation that Emma was attractive. He'd always *known* she was attractive. Dan Morgan wouldn't be seen dating a moose, even for business reasons. That didn't mean she was his type, though—not with her dark hair and minimal make-up, and her conservative taste in clothes. And that in turn had made it easy to pigeon-hole her as friend. A proper relationship with someone like Emma would be complex, would need commitment, compromise, emotional investment. All things he wasn't prepared to give another woman. Tried, tested and failed. Dan Morgan learned from his mistakes and never repeated his failures.

It had quickly become clear that Emma was far more useful to him in the role of friend than love interest, and all thoughts of attraction had been relegated from that moment onwards. It had been so long now that not noticing the way she looked was second nature.

But the gnawing feeling in his gut was there nonetheless. Their romantic relationship might have been counterfeit, but some element of it had obviously been real enough to make the dumping feel extremely uncomfortable.

He'd never been dumped before. *He* was the one who did the backing off. That was the way he played it. A couple of dinner dates somewhere nice, the second one generally ending up in his bed, a couple more dates and then, when the girl started to show signs of getting comfortable—maybe she'd start leaving belongings in his flat, or perhaps she'd suggest he meet her family—he'd simply go into backing-off mode. It wasn't as if he lied to them about his intentions. He was careful always to make it clear from the outset that he wasn't in the market for anything serious. He was in absolute control at all times—just as he was in every aspect of his life. That was the way he wanted it. The way he *needed* it.

He was amazed at how affronted he felt by the apparent ease with which Emma had dispensed with him. Not an ounce of concern for how *he* might feel as she'd planned to trounce him spectacularly in front of all those people. His irritation at her unbelievable fake break-up plan was surpassed only by his anger with himself for actually giving a damn.

Feeling low at being dumped meant you had feelings for the person dumping you. Didn't it?

Unease flared in his gut at that needling thought, because Dan Morgan didn't *do* deep feelings. That slippery slope led to dark places he had no intention of revisiting. He did fun, easy, no-strings flings. Feelings need not apply. Surely hurt feelings should only apply where a relationship was bona fide. Fake relationships should mean fake feelings, and fake feelings couldn't be hurt.

That sensation of spinning back in time made him feel faintly nauseous. Here it was again—like an irritating old acquaintance you think you've cut out of your life who then pops back up unexpectedly for a visit.

That reeling loss of control he'd felt in the hideous few months after Maggie had left, walking away with apparent ease from the ruins of their relationship. He'd made sure he retained the upper hand in all dealings with women since. These days every situation worked for *him*. No emotion involved. No risk. His relationships were orchestrated by *him*, no one else. That way he could be sure of every outcome.

But not this time. Their agreement had lasted—what?—a year? And in that time she'd never once refused a date with him. Even when he'd needed an escort at the last minute she'd changed her schedule to accommodate him. He'd relied on her because he'd learned that he *could* rely on her.

And so he hadn't seen it coming. That was why it gnawed at him like this.

You don't like losing her. You thought you had her on your own terms. You took her for granted and now you don't like the feeling that she's calling the shots.

He gritted his teeth. This smacked a bit too much of the past for comfort. It resurrected old feelings that he had absolutely no desire to recall, and he apparently couldn't let it slide. What he needed to do now was get this thing back under his own control.

Well, she hadn't gone yet. And he didn't have to just *take* her decision. If this agreement was going to end it would be when *he* chose—not on some whim of hers. He could talk her round if he wanted to. It wouldn't be hard. And then *he* would decide where their partnership went.

If it went anywhere at all.

He pulled his chair back close to the desk and pressed a few buttons, bringing up his calendar for the next couple of weeks with a stab of exasperation. Had she no idea of the inconvenience she'd thrust upon him?

Not only had Emma dumped him, she'd really picked a great moment to do it. *Not.* The black tie charity dinner a week away hadn't crossed his mind the other evening when she had dropped her bombshell. It hadn't needed to. Since he'd met Emma planning for events like that had been a thing of the past. He simply called her up, sometimes at no more than a moment's notice, and he could count on the perfect companion on his arm— perfect respect for the dress code, perfect intelligent conversation, an all-round perfect professional impression. There was some serious networking to be had at such an event, the tickets had cost a fortune, and now he was dateless.

He reached for the phone.

It rang for so long that he was on the brink of hanging up when she answered.

'Hello?' Her slightly husky voice sounded breathless, as if she'd just finished laughing at something, and he could hear music and buzzing talk in the background, as if she were in a crowded bar or restaurant.

From nowhere three unheard-of things flashed through his mind in quick succession. Emma never socialised on a work night unless she was with him; she never let her phone ring for long when he called her, as if she was eager to talk to him; and in the time that he'd known her she had never sounded this bubblingly happy.

'What are you doing a week from Friday?' he said, cutting to the chase.

'Hang on.'

A brief pause on the end of the phone and the blaring music was muted a little. He imagined her leaving the bar or the restaurant she was in for a quiet spot, perhaps in the lobby. He sensed triumph already, knowing that she was leaving whoever she was with to make time to speak with *him*.

'Tying up loose ends at work, probably. And packing.'

So she was storming ahead with her plans, then. The need for control spiked again in his gut. He went in with the big guns.

'I've got a charity ball in Mayfair. Black tie. Major league. Tickets like hen's teeth. It promises to be a fabulous night.'

He actually heard her sigh. With impatience, or with longing at the thought of attending the ball with him? He decided it was definitely the latter. She'd made no secret of the fact she enjoyed the wonderful opulence of nights like that, and he knew she'd networked a good few new clients for herself in the past while she was accompanying him—another perk of their plus-one agreement.

For Pete's sake, she had him giving it that ludicrous name now.

Their usual dates consisted of restaurant dinners with his clients. Pleasant, but hardly exciting. Except for Dan's own company, of course. Luxury events like this only came up occasionally. He waited for her to tear his arm off in her eagerness to accept.

'What part of "it's over" did you not understand, Dan?' she said. 'Did you not hear any of what I said the other night?'

It took a moment to process what she'd said because he had been so convinced of her acceptance.

'What I heard was some insane plan to desert your whole life as you know it for some guy you've known five minutes,' he heard himself say. 'You're talking about leaving your friends and family, walking out of a job you've worked your arse off for, all to follow some celebrity.'

'It would be a sabbatical from work,' she said. 'I'm not burning my bridges there. Not yet. And you make me sound like some crazy stalker. We're in a relationship. A proper grown-up one, not a five-minute fling.'

He didn't miss the obvious dig at his own love life, and it made his response more cutting than he intended.

'On the strength of—what was it?—*half a dozen dates?*' he said. 'I always thought you were one of the most grounded people I know. You're the last person in the world I'd have expected to be star-struck.'

He knew from the freezing silence on the end of the phone that he'd sunk his foot into his own mouth up to the ankle.

'How dare you?' she said, and a light tremble laced her voice, which was pure frost. 'It was obviously too much to hope that you might actually be *pleased* for me. Yes, Alistair is in the public eye, but that has *nothing* to do with why I've agreed to go away with him. Has it occurred to you that I might actually like him because he's interested in *me* for a change? As opposed to the grandchildren I might bear him or the fact I might be his carer when he's old and decrepit. Or…' she added pointedly '…the fact that I might boost his profile at some damned work dinner so he can extend his client list a bit further because he never quite feels he's rich or successful enough.'

She paused.

'You're saying no, then?' he said. 'To the all-expenses-paid top-notch Mayfair ball?'

He heard her draw in a huge breath and then she let

it out in a rude, exasperated noise. He held the phone briefly away from his ear. When he put it back her voice was Arctic.

'Dan,' she was saying slowly, as if he had a problem understanding plain English, 'I'm saying no to the Mayfair ball. I'm through with posing as your professional romantic interest so you can impress your damned client list while you date airhead models for a week at a time.'

Had he really thought this would be easy? It occurred to him that in reality she couldn't be further from one of his usual conquests, of which currently there were two or three, any of whom would drop everything else at a moment's notice if he deigned to call them up and suggest getting together.

You didn't get as far up the legal career ladder as she had by being a 'yes' girl. But her easy refusal bothered the hell out of him. He'd expected her to agree to resurrect their agreement without even needing persuasion. Had expected her to thank him, in fact.

The need to win back control rose another notch with her unexpected refusal of his offer, and also her apparent indifference to it. It put his teeth on edge and gnawed at him deep inside.

'How about helping me out with this one last time, then?' he pressed, confident that in an evening he could quickly turn the situation around. Reinstate their agreement and then decide what he wanted to do with it. End it, change the terms—whatever happened it would be up to him to decide, *not* her.

'Dan, you don't need my help,' she said patiently. 'I'm in the middle of dinner and I haven't got time to discuss this now. It's not as if you're short of dates. Grab your little black book and pick one of your girlies from there. I'm sure any one of them would love to go with you.'

There was a soft click on the end of the phone as she hung up.

That went well. *Not.*

CHAPTER THREE

'LET ME JUST recap. You're in a relationship with Alistair Woods—*the* Alistair Woods, the man who looks a dream in Lycra—and you're not planning on mentioning it to Mum and Dad?'

Adam's eyebrows practically disappeared into his sleek quiff hairstyle and Emma took a defensive sip of coffee. The fantasy she'd had of disappearing around the world on Alistair's arm and calling up her parents from Cannes/LA/somewhere else that screamed kudos, to tell them she would be featuring in next month's celebrity magazine, had turned out to be just that. A fantasy.

Because Adam was getting married.

Her big brother, Adam—who never failed to make her laugh, and who was so bright and sharp and funny that she'd never for a moment questioned her role in family life as the forgettable backing act to his flamboyant scene-stealer. Of *course* she had paled into insignificance in her family's eyes next to Adam—not to mention in the eyes of schoolteachers, friends, neighbours… But only in the way that everyone else had faded into the background next to him in her own eyes. He was simply someone who commanded success and attention without needing to put in any effort.

She couldn't exit her life without telling Adam, and she'd asked him to meet her for coffee to do exactly that. She'd even tried to sweeten the news by buying him an enormous cream bun, which now sat between them untouched. If she'd thought he'd simply scoff the bun and wave her off without so much as a question, she'd been deluded.

'You're not going yet, though, right? You're at least waiting until after the wedding?'

'Erm…'

He threw his arms up theatrically.

'Em! You can't be serious! How the hell am I going to keep Mum under control without you? I can't get married without my wingman!'

'Woman,' she corrected.

He flapped both hands at her madly.

'Whatever. You saw what Mum was like the other night. The wedding is in Ernie's home village. He's got a massive family, they're all fabulously supportive, and if you don't come along our family's big impression on them will be Mum telling everyone I'll get over it when I get bored with musical theatre and meet the right girl.'

'Dad will be there,' she ventured. 'Maybe you could talk to him beforehand, get him to keep Mum on a short leash.'

'He'd be as much use as a chocolate teapot. We both know he's been beaten into submission over the years. Since when has Mum ever listened to him? She just talks over him. I *need* you there.'

His voice had taken on a pleading tone.

'It's not as simple as that. Alistair's covering another cycling race in a few weeks' time. We're meant to be having a break before it starts because it's pretty full-on. I'm flying out to the States, meeting some of his friends and family, relaxing for a couple of weeks. It's all been arranged.'

She looked down at her coffee cup because she couldn't bear the disappointment on Adam's face.

Adam had never made her feel insignificant. Any inability to measure up was her failing, not his. And she was the one who let it bother her.

'Then there's no problem! Bring Alistair to the wedding,' Adam said, clapping his hands together excitedly. 'You've already said he's got time off from work. The guy's probably got a private jet. You could zoom in and zoom out on the same day if you had to.' He made a soaring aeroplane motion in the air with his hand.

She suppressed a mirthless laugh.

'You mean introduce him to Mum and Dad? A whole new person for Mum to drive insane?' She narrowed suspicious eyes at him. 'It would certainly take the heat off you and Ernie.'

He held his hands up.

'You'll have to introduce him at some point anyway. OK, so you might travel with him for a while, maybe even settle in the States with him, but you'll have to come home to visit, won't you?'

She didn't answer. Visiting wasn't something she'd thought about much in her excitement about getting away. It hadn't crossed her mind that she'd be missed that much.

'Bloody hell, Em.'

She sighed. She couldn't say no to Adam any more than the rest of the world could. He just had that gift.

'It'll be a nightmare if I bring Alistair,' she said. 'Mum will be all over him like a rash, demanding marriage and grandchildren and mentioning my biological clock. He's a free spirit. He'll run a bloody mile.'

Adam was on the comment like a shot.

'Then you definitely *should* bring him. You're talking about leaving your whole life behind to be with him— don't you think he ought to prove himself a bit before you take that kind of plunge? If he's really the guy you think he is—if he's really going to put you first above everything else in his life—then he'll love you no matter what crazy relative you introduce him to, right?'

She couldn't help latching on to that thought—that desire for a level of regard where she would come absolutely first with someone for a change. Was that what this was really about? Was she afraid to bring Alistair to the wedding because of some stupid subconscious conviction that he might see through her? Might see that she really was a plain and inferior mousy girl, despite all the years she'd put in on breaking away from that persona?

'He does love me,' she insisted, mainly to bat away the prickle of unease that had begun in her stomach. It was all Adam's fault for questioning her perfectly laid plans.

'Great. Then put your man where your mouth is. Introduce him to Mum and watch him prove it.'

Dan clicked his phone off with ill-suppressed irritation.

Cancelling a working lunch at a moment's notice was extremely bad form. Focused to a pinpoint on work performance himself, he found it difficult to tolerate lateness or bad planning in others. Especially when it meant he'd interrupted his day to turn up at a restaurant when he could have eaten lunch on the run or at his desk.

He gave the menu an uninterested glance and was on

the point of calling for the bill for the two drinks he'd ordered while waiting for the no-show client when he saw Emma cross the restaurant. A waiter showed her to a table by the window and she sat down alone, so engrossed in scrolling through her phone that she didn't even notice he was in the room.

The news that she was leaving seemed to have given him a new heightened perspective, and he picked up on tiny details about her that had simply passed him by before. He saw her objectively for once, as someone else might. Alistair Woods, for example. This time his gaze skimmed over her usual business dress when previously it would have stopped at observing the sharply cut grey suit. Instead he now noticed how slender she was. How had he never picked up before on the striking contrast of her double cream skin with her dark hair? The ripe fullness of her lower lip? When you had reason to look past the sensible work image she was unexpectedly cute. He'd been so busy taking her presence for granted he'd failed to notice any of those things.

Maybe this lunchtime wouldn't be a total waste of time after all. Dealing with her on the phone had been a bad choice. A face-to-face meeting might be a better approach to talking sense into her.

He picked up his drink and crossed the room towards her. His stomach gave a sudden flutter that made him pause briefly en route to the table—then he remembered that it was lunchtime. He was obviously just hungry, and since he was here maybe he should take the chance to grab a sandwich as well as a drink and a smoothing-over session with her. Not that his appetite had been up to much this last week or so.

'Dan!'

Her eyes widened in surprise as he slid into the seat opposite her and put his drink down on the table. She glanced quickly around the restaurant, presumably for a waiter.

'Really glad I bumped into you,' he said. 'Just wanted to say no hard feelings about the other night.'

A smile touched the corner of her lips, drawing his eyes there. She was wearing a light pink lipstick that gave them a delectable soft sheen.

'The other night?' she said.

'The charity ball.'

'I hadn't realised there *could* be hard feelings,' she said, toying with her water glass. 'It was just a work arrangement we had after all, right? Not like I broke off a date, is it?'

She held his gaze steadily and for the first time it occurred to him that it might take a bit more than sweet-talking for him to regain the advantage between them. His own fault, of course. He was judging her by the standards of his usual dates, who seemed to fall over themselves to hang on his every word. Emma was a different ball game altogether. Taking her for granted had been a mistake.

He gestured to the waiter for a menu.

'How did it go, then?' she said.

'How did what go?' he evaded.

'The charity ball?' she said. 'No-expenses-spared Mayfair hotel, wasn't it? Who did you take?'

'Eloise,' he said shortly.

She had to bring it up, didn't she? When what he'd really like would be to erase the entire evening from history.

'Which one's that?'

She cranked her hand in a come-on gesture and looked at him expectantly until he elaborated.

'She's a leg model,' he said. 'You know—tights, stockings, that kind of thing.'

The woman had the best legs in the business. Unfortunately she was entirely defined by that one physical feature. Tact, sense and reliability didn't come into it.

'Did you make any new contacts?' Emma said. 'Normally charity bashes are great for networking, aren't they? Perfect opportunity for a shared goal, loads of rich businessmen?'

'Normally they are,' he said. 'But normally I have you with me, oozing tact and diplomacy and class.'

It had been kind of hard to hold a professional conversation with Eloise's arms wound constantly around his neck like a long-legged monkey. The one time he had begun to make headway with a potential client she'd returned from the bar with two flutes of pink champagne and positioned herself between them by sitting on his lap.

He watched Emma carefully, to see if his compliment had hit its mark, and was rewarded with the lightest of rosy blushes touching her high cheekbones. Hah! Not so easily dismissed after all. A proper in-depth talk about her whirlwind plans and he was confident he could sow a few seeds of doubt. From there it would be a short step to convincing her to stay put, reinstating their working agreement, getting things back to normal.

He was giving her a quick follow-up smile when he realised her eyes were actually focused somewhere over his shoulder and the blush had nothing to do with him. A wide smile lit up her face and suddenly she was on her feet, being drawn into a kiss by a tall blond man with a deep golden tan and perfect white teeth. No matter that he was wearing a sharply cut designer suit and an open-necked silk shirt instead of clinging Lycra cycling shorts and a helmet. He was instantly recognisable—by Dan and by the room at large.

Alistair Woods was on the premises.

The surrounding tables suddenly appeared to be filled with rubberneckers. Clearly basking in the attention, he offered a wave and a nod of greeting to the tables either side of them before sitting down—as if he was a film star instead of a has-been athlete. Dan felt an irrational lurch of dislike for the guy, whom he'd never met before but who clearly made Emma brim with happiness.

Jealous? his mind whispered.

He dismissed the thought out of hand. This wasn't about jealousy. Emma was clearly star-struck and on the brink of making a rash decision that could ruin her working life and her personal life before you could say *yellow jersey*. If anything, he would be doing her a favour by bringing her back down to earth.

'Alistair, this is Dan,' Emma said, taking her seat again, her hand entwined in Alistair's. 'Dan, this is Alistair Woods.'

She glanced pointedly at Dan.

'Dan happened to be here meeting someone,' she said. 'He just came over to say hello.'

She didn't want him to join them. It couldn't be clearer.

'Heard a lot about you, friend,' Alistair said in a strong American accent, stretching in his seat. 'You're the platonic plus-one, right?'

Of all the qualities he possessed that Emma could choose to reference him by she'd chosen that. Just *great*.

'Did you get my phone message?' Emma asked Alistair eagerly. 'I know it means rejigging our plans a little, but I just can't let my brother down. It's his wedding day. And it'll be a good chance for you to meet my family.'

She was taking Alistair to Adam's civil partnership ceremony?

Dan felt a deep and lurching stab of misplaced envy at the thought of this guy slotting neatly into his recently vacated place—fake though it might have been—in regard to Emma's family. OK, so they were opinionated and mouthy, and in her mother's case that translated as being downright bigoted at times, but he'd never felt anything but welcomed by them, and their simple mad chaos had been something he'd enjoyed.

An unhappy flash of his own childhood rose in his mind. His mother, hardly more than a child herself. No father—at least not in any way that mattered to a kid. Plenty of 'uncles', though. He hadn't been short of those. And plenty of random babysitters—friends of his mother's, neighbours, hardly the same person twice. What he wouldn't have given for an interfering nosy mother at the age of thirteen, when babysitters had no longer been required and he'd been considered old enough to be left home alone.

He dismissed the thought. Things were different now. He'd learned to rely only on himself, without influence from anyone else. Maggie had been the one time he'd deviated from that course, and it had turned out to be an agonising mistake that he had no intention of repeating. He had no need for family. Past or future.

'Got your message, baby, but there's no way we're going to be able to make the gay wedding,' Alistair said.

Dan watched Emma's smile falter and suppressed an unexpected urge to grab Woods by the scruff of the neck.

'Why not?' she said. 'I can't miss Adam's wedding. I promised him.'

Dan recognised her tone as carefully neutral. She was upset and trying to cover it up. Did this Alistair know her well enough to pick up that little nuance? *Hardly.*

Emma took a sip of her coffee in an effort to hide her disappointment. Had she really thought it would be that simple? That he would just agree to her every whim?

'We're spending that weekend in the Hamptons,' Alistair was saying. 'I've been in talks to land a movie role and one of the producers is having a garden party. Can't miss it. Lots riding on it. I'm sure Arnold will understand. Career first, right?' He leaned in towards her with a winning expression and squeezed her hand. 'We agreed.'

His career first.

'Adam,' Emma corrected. She could hear the disappointment, cold and heavy, in her own voice. 'His name is Adam. And I really *can't* miss his wedding.'

Alistair sat back and released her hand, leaving it lying abandoned in the middle of the white tablecloth. His irritation was instant and palpable, and all the more of a shock because he'd never been anything but sweetness and light so far. But then, she hadn't demanded anything from him so far, had she? She'd been only too eager to go along for the ride. *His* ride.

'You do whatever you have to do, baby,' he said dismissively. 'You can fly out and join me afterwards.'

'But I really wanted you to be there, to meet my family.'

'Sorry, honey, no can do.'

Alistair turned to the waiter to order a drink. She noticed that Dan was looking at her with sympathy and she looked away. Everything was unravelling and it was a million times worse because he was here to witness it. She tried to muster up an attitude that might smother the churning disappointment in her stomach as her high hopes plummeted.

From the moment she'd met Alistair he had made her feel special, as if nothing was too much trouble for him. But it occurred to her that it had only related to peripheral things, like flowers and restaurants and which hotel they might stay in. Now it had come down to something that was truly important to her he hadn't delivered the goods. It wasn't even up for discussion. Because it clashed with his own plans.

Disappointment mingled hideously with exasperated disbelief. She felt like crashing her head down despairingly on the table. Would she ever, at any point in her life, meet someone who might actually put her first on their agenda? Or was this her lot? To make her way through life as some lower down priority?

'Look, I don't want to interfere,' Dan said suddenly, leaning forward. 'But how about I step in?'

'What do you mean, step in?' she asked, eyes narrowed.

Suspicion. Not a good sign, Dan thought. On the other hand Alistair was looking more than open to the suggestion.

Dispensing with Alistair to some swanky party on a different continent was far too good an opportunity to pass up. All he needed to do was step into Alistair's shoes as Emma's date and he'd have a whole weekend to make her rethink her actions and to get the situation working for him again.

'I got my invitation to the wedding this morning,' he said, thinking of the gaudy card that had arrived in the post, with *'Groom & Groom!'* plastered across the front in bright yellow, very much in keeping with Adam's usual in-your-face style.

'*You've* been invited?' she asked with obvious surprise, as if their interaction had been so fake that all the connections he'd made with her family were counterfeit, too. But he genuinely liked Adam—they'd always had a laugh.

'Yes,' he said. 'So if Alistair is away working I can fill in if you like—escort you. It's not as if I haven't done it before. What do you think?'

She stared at him.

'For old times' sake?' he pressed. 'I'm sure Alistair won't mind.'

He glanced at the ex-cyclist, who held his hands up.

'Great idea!' he said. 'Problem solved.'

Emma's face was inscrutable.

'That won't be necessary,' she snapped. 'And actually, Dan, if you don't mind, we could do with a bit of time to talk this over.'

She looked at him expectantly and when he didn't move raised impatient eyebrows and nodded her head imperceptibly towards the door.

All was no longer peachy with her and Mr Perfect and that meant opportunity. He should be ecstatic. All he needed to do was leave them be and let the idiot drive a wedge between them, because one thing he knew about Emma was that her parents might drive her up the pole but Adam meant the world to her. Yet his triumph was somehow diluted by a surge of protectiveness towards Emma at Alistair's easy dismissal of her. He had to force himself not to give the smug idiot a piece of his mind.

He made himself stand up and excused himself from the table.

Give the guy enough leeway and he would alienate Emma all by himself. Dan could call her up later in the role of concerned friend and reinstate their agreement on his own terms.

Bumped to make room for Alistair's career?

Her mind insisted on recycling Adam's comments from the day before. *'Don't you think he ought to prove himself before you take that kind of plunge?'* Was it really so much to ask?

The insistent 'case closed' way Alistair had refused her suggestion told her far more about him than just his words alone, and it occurred to her in a crushing blow of clarity. How had she ever thought she would come first with someone who had an ego the size of Alistair's? An ego which was still growing, by the sound of it, if he was trying to break into the movies.

The waiter brought their food and she watched as Alistair tucked in with gusto to an enormous steak and side salad, oblivious to the fact that there was anything wrong between them. He'd got his own way. For him it was business as usual. His whole attitude now irked her. It was as if she should be somehow grateful for being invited along for the ride. She'd been too busy being swept away by the excitement of someone like him actually taking an interest in her to comprehend that being with him would mean giving up her life in favour of his. Where the hell did she come first in all of that?

It dawned on her that he'd have a lot of contractual issues coming his way with his broadening career. Was that what made her attractive to him? The way she dealt so efficiently with legal red tape on his behalf? Had he earmarked her as his own live-in source of legal advice?

This wasn't a relationship; it was an *agreement*. All she'd done was swap one for another. She could be Dan's platonic plus-one or Alistair's live-in lawyer. Where the hell was the place for what *she* wanted in any of that?

'It's all off, Alistair,' she said dully. It felt as if her voice was coming from somewhere else.

He peered at her hardly touched plate of food.

'What is, honey? The fish?'

He looked around for a waiter while she marvelled at his self-assurance that her sentence couldn't possibly relate to their relationship. Not in *his* universe. Alistair probably had a queue of women desperate to date him, all of them a zillion times more attractive than Emma. He had international travel, a beach home in Malibu, a little getaway in the Balearics, his own restaurant and a glittering media career in his corner. What the hell did she have that could compete with that? Interfering parents and a tiny flat in Putney? Why the hell would he think she might want to back out?

'Us,' she said. 'You and me. It's not going to work out.'

He gaped at her.

'Is this because I won't come to your gay brother's wedding? Honey, have you any idea how much is riding on this new contract? This is the next stage of my career we're talking about.' He shook his head at her in a gesture of amazement. 'The effort that's gone into lining up this meeting. I'm not cancelling that so you can show me off to your relatives at some small-town pink wedding. And it's not as if I'm stopping you going. That Neanderthal platonic pal of yours has said he'll step up to the plate.'

She was vaguely aware of people staring with interest from the surrounding tables. His slight about Dan irked her. Neanderthal? Hardly. He looked like an Adonis, and he was smart, sharp and funny. She clenched her teeth defensively on his behalf.

'I want *you* to come with me. I want you to meet my family.'

'And I will, honey. When the time's right.'

'It's a family wedding. Everyone who knows me will be in one place for the first time in years. When could the time possibly be more right than that?'

His face changed. Subtly but instantly. Like the turning of a switch. The easy, open look that had really taken her in when she'd first met him, the way he'd listened to her as if she mattered and showed her real, genuine interest, was gone. That look was now replaced by a sulky, petulant frown.

'Because it's all about *you,* of course,' he said. 'No regard for *my* career. You have to make these opportunities, Emma, and then follow them up. You don't mess people like this about, because there are no second chances. I can't believe you're being so selfish.'

For a moment the Emma she'd grown up to be actually questioned her own judgement on the strength of that last comment of his. The insecure Emma, whom she'd begun to push out of her life when she'd at last moved away from home and gone to university—a place where she had finally been accepted without reference to Adam or anyone else. With her own successes not watered down but recognised. After university she'd moved to London instead of going home to the West Country, in case that old, pessimistic Emma was somehow still there, lurking, ready to take over.

No way was she going back to *that* mindset now.

She pushed her plate to one side and leaned down to pick up her bag and take out her purse. She took enough money to cover her own meal and put it down on the table. She didn't throw it down. She wasn't going to resort to stupid tantrum gestures—she was a professional.

'I'm sorry, Alistair.' She shook her head at him. 'I don't know what I was thinking. I thought there would be more to us than being driven by your career. You want me to travel with you so I can iron out your legal issues, don't you? Maybe draw up the odd contract, or just hand out advice where you need it?'

He didn't say anything.

'Come on—be honest with me. Is that what this has really been about?'

A long pause.

'Well, you can't deny it's an advantage,' he said eventually. 'But only in the same way as if you were a hairdresser or a stylist.'

'I thought we were having a relationship. I didn't realise I was joining your entourage,' she snapped. 'I should never have let myself get swept away by this. Have a nice trip back to the States.'

She left the table and aimed her shaky feet at the exit, determined not to look back. When she did, inevitably, she saw that he was signing autographs for the people at an adjacent table. No attempt to follow her or talk her round. But why would he? He undoubtedly had a queue of people waiting to take her place.

She pressed her teeth hard together and concentrated on them to take her mind off the ache in her heart and the even worse heat of stupidity in her face.

She'd bigged up her relationship with him beyond all reason. How could she have been such a fool?

Now she had to face the climb down.

CHAPTER FOUR

EMMA GLANCED AROUND the half-empty office, grateful that her colleagues had finally drifted out for lunch. She'd informed HR first thing that her new, glamorous life as the jet-set girlfriend of Alistair 'White Lightning' Woods was no longer happening and the news had quickly filtered through the staff. At least she hadn't jacked her job in completely. That would have made things a whole lot worse. And it was best to get the humiliation over with, right?

Except that she wasn't sure how many more sympathetic stares she could take.

Her phone blared into life and she looked down at the display screen.

Dan. Again.

She pressed her hot forehead with the heel of one hand, as if it might help her think clearly. There'd been rather a lack of clear thinking around her lately.

What the hell had possessed her to let Alistair Woods sweep her off her feet? She was a sensible professional. She knew her own mind and she never took risks. Was she so bogged down in a stupid teen inferiority complex, in a lifetime of failed one-upmanship with Adam, that she'd momentarily lost all common sense? She'd built a life here in London, where she blended in. She'd excelled at not being noticeable and her professional life had flourished. And now, the one time she'd ventured out of that safe box, the same old outcome had happened. Her judgement had been rubbish, she hadn't measured up and it had all come crashing down around her ears. Why had she ever thought things would be different with Alistair?

Defensive heat rose in her cheeks even as she picked up the phone. By extreme bad luck Dan had been there in the restaurant to see that her romance with Alistair wasn't such a bed of roses after all. The thought of filling him in on all the details made a wave of nausea rise in her throat and her eyes water.

'Hello.' She shaped her voice into the most neutral tone she could muster.

'Hey.'

His voice was warm, deep and full of concern, and her heart gave a little flutter because as a rule Dan Morgan didn't do concern. He did sharply professional business demands, he did high expectations, he did arm's length.

'Just checking that you're OK.'

I blabbed to everyone who knows me in London that I was on the point of eloping with the most desirable man in sport. I've made the biggest fool of myself and now I have to tell everyone that, actually, he's an arse and it's not going ahead. So, yes, thanks, I'm just peachy.

Climbing down in front of Dan was somehow worst of all. And not just because she was embarrassed at her own poor judgement when she should have known better. There was a tiny part of her mind that was busy pointing out that for the first time ever Dan was showing interest and support for her beyond what she could do for him and his work. Had he suddenly realised he valued her as more than just a handy plus-one? How many missed calls from him had she had since lunchtime? Five? Wasn't that a bit excessive?

'Why wouldn't I be?' she said.

'Things just seemed a little tense at lunch yesterday.'

As if you could cut the atmosphere with a chainsaw.

'Did you get everything sorted with Alistair?'

A rush of bitterness pelted through her as she answered. 'Oh, yes. I *definitely* got everything sorted with him.'

'He's changed his plans, then? He's coming to the civil partnership?'

Oh, bloody hell, the civil partnership.

An unsettling wave of trepidation turned her stomach over. The biggest Burney family get-together in years and she no longer had a date. Could her crushed and battered ego survive a whole weekend of jibes from her mother about the race for grandchildren being hampered by her inability to keep a man?

'Not exactly,' she said.

'How do you mean?'

There was a sharp over-interested edge to his voice that she recognised from the many work dinners she'd accompanied him to. This was how he sounded when he was on the brink of nailing a new client—as if nothing could distract him from his goal. *Five missed calls and now he was hanging on her every word.*

Oh, hell.

She leaned forward over the desk in exasperation and pressed her hot forehead against its cold wooden surface.

'Alistair and I are off,' she blurted out. 'He's a total *arse*. He wouldn't even talk about making it to the wedding.'

'You broke up because he won't come to your brother's wedding?'

'Pretty much, yes,' she said.

She couldn't bring herself to tell him the truth—that Alistair had only treated her like a princess because he'd wanted a live-in lawyer. Her cheeks burned just at the thought of it.

'I couldn't let Adam down and he just couldn't see that. It made me realise that work will always come first for him.'

'Sorry to hear that.'

Was there a twist of cool I-told-you-so about his voice? She pulled her head from the desk and narrowed her eyes, trying to decide. He was probably glad it was all off. Wasn't that exactly what he'd wanted? For things to get back to normal? Then again, at least he wasn't saying it out loud.

She tightened her grip on the phone.

Wallowing in self-pity was one thing, but it didn't change the fact that in a week's time she had to keep her parents in check while surrounded by Ernie's family. Knowing Adam, it would be the most stuffed-with-people event of the year. She'd become so used to relying on Dan at family get-togethers that the prospect of coping with that by herself filled her with dread.

With her dreams in tatters there was a warm tug of temptation just to scuttle back to the way things had been. And wasn't that exactly what Dan had been angling for all along? Why not resurrect the old plus-one agreement? That nice, safe social buffer that had stood between her and humiliation until she'd stupidly given it up. Her reason for ending it was on its way back to the States right now. She'd dipped a toe in the murky waters of proper dating and it had turned into a train wreck.

She thought it through quickly. Dan was brilliant with her mother, never remotely fazed and the epitome of calm. Exactly what she needed to get her through that scary event. And maybe then she could begin to look forward, put Alistair behind her, make a fresh start.

'Actually, about the wedding…' she said.

'You want to reinstate the plus-one agreement?' He might as well give it its proper ludicrous name.

'Yes. I know it's a bit of a turnaround.'

Just a bit.

He couldn't quite believe his ears. So *now* she wanted him to step back in as her handy fake boyfriend, as if the last couple of weeks had never happened? What about her insane plan to dump him in public? And she hadn't done him the one-off favour of going with him to his Mayfair charity ball—oh, no. He'd had to spend the evening peeling Eloise off him. But *now* she needed *him* things were different.

And he wasn't about to make it easy for her.

'I thought having each other as a social backup was *holding us back?*' he said. 'Your words.'

A pause on the end of the phone, during which a hint of triumph coursed through him as he reclaimed the upper hand. He was back in control. How they proceeded from here would be *his* decision, not hers.

'I may have been a bit hasty.'

He didn't answer.

'Please, Dan. Ernie has a massive family and his father's a High Court Judge. Our family is me and my parents plus a few distant relatives that my mother's alienated over the years. I've promised Adam I'll keep my mum in check, and the thought of doing it on my own fills me with horror. *Please.* You're so good with them.'

She paused again, and when he didn't immediately leap in to agree, deployed the big guns of guilt.

'I thought this was what you wanted—everything back the way it was? I know I screwed up, and I'm sorry. But how many times have I helped *you* out at the last minute? What about that race meet where you landed your biggest client? You called me two hours before and I stepped in. Won't you even consider doing this one tiny event for me?'

He hesitated. She had a point about the race meet.

'Please, Dan. I want to make sure everything runs smoothly for Adam. You know how hard it is to please my mother.'

She'd lowered her voice now and a pang of sympathy twisted in his gut because he *did* know.

He could tell from her defeated tone that she thought he was going to refuse. This was his opportunity to bring things right back to where he wanted them. Their agreement had paid dividends—there was no denying that—but he'd let it run on far too long. He'd become complacent and let her become too important to drop easily. He couldn't have someone like that in his life, even if it *was* supposed to be under the heading of 'work'. She wanted a fake boyfriend for the wedding? He'd be the best fake boyfriend in the world. For old times' sake. And then he'd dump their agreement without looking back for a second.

'OK,' he said.

Emma took a deep breath as sweet relief flooded her. It had absolutely nothing to do with the prospect of Dan's company of course. She was way past that. It was just the thought of having an ally in what was bound to be a social minefield.

'Really?' she said. 'I wasn't sure you'd agree after I said no to your charity thing. Thank you *so* much. And you know I'm happy to step in next time you need someone—'

'Please let me finish,' he cut in. 'I'll do it. But this is the last time. I'll stand in for you in acknowledgement of all the times you've stepped in for me at the last minute. But when we head back to London after the wedding, that's it. Our agreement is over. I'll manage my own socialising going forward, and you can carry on as before.'

Emma took a sharp breath, because for some reason that hurt in a way that the Alistair debacle hadn't. He didn't sound inclined even to retain a friendship between them. They would revert to being Mr Morgan and Ms Burney, businessman and lawyer, nothing more. Had she really meant so little to him?

It was a stupid, stupid pang of disappointment because she'd already *dealt* with the idea that nothing would ever happen between her and Dan. Her ridiculous crush on him was a thing of the past. She'd been planning to travel the world with Alistair, for Pete's sake, never looking back.

It had somehow been much easier to deal with when *she'd* been the one making that choice.

Emma glanced around the lobby of the Cotswolds hotel that Adam and Ernie had chosen as their wedding venue, surprised at the stunning old-world charm of the place.

Huge vases of spring flowers softened the dark wood panelling of the walls. Beautifully upholstered chairs and sofas stood in cosy groupings around the fireplace, which was taller than she was.

She would have expected Adam to want to make his vows somewhere screamingly modern in the midst of the buzz of London. Apparently Ernie's family were a lot more old-school than that. They'd lived here in this honey-coloured stone village for generations. She felt a stab of envy at the give and take in her brother's relationship. It seemed *Adam* didn't have a problem putting his partner's family first.

On the other hand it might have been less nerve-racking if the wedding *was* taking place on home ground. Here they would be surrounded by Ernie's nearest and dearest, all eagerly awaiting the impression the Burney family would make. Her stomach gave a churn of unease at the thought.

'What name is it?'

The blonde receptionist ran a manicured fingernail down her computer screen.

'Burney,' Emma said. 'I'm part of the Burney-Harford wedding party.'

Adam had made a block reservation.

Dan strode through the door, fresh from parking the car. He rested one hand on the desk and ran the other through his dark hair, spiking it more than ever. His blue eyes crinkled as he smiled his gorgeous lopsided smile— the one that had melted half the female hearts in London.

The manicured fingernail came to an instant stand-still and the receptionist's jaw practically fell open as she gazed at him.

'Mr and Mrs Burney?' she asked.

Emma sighed.

'No, that would be my parents.' Mercifully they weren't here yet. 'It will be under Miss.'

The girl handed over keys—proper old-fashioned ones—and a wad of check-in paperwork.

Emma gave Dan an expectant look.

He smiled at her.

'Great venue.'

'What about you?' she said.

'What *about* me?'

'Your booking,' she whispered.

In her peripheral vision she picked up the interested change in the receptionist's posture. She'd seen it a hundred times before. She took in her appearance. Blonde hair—*check*. Sleekly made-up face—*check*. Eager smile—*check*. She knew exactly what would come next.

She waited for Dan to confirm loudly that he had a separate booking—ergo, he was free and single, and in possession of a hotel room and a shedload of charm. Instead he held her own gaze steadily, as if his radar no longer picked up pretty blondes. Not a hint of a flirt or smoulder. Not so much as a glance in the girl's direction.

'Didn't make one,' he said cheerfully.

Emma stared at him incredulously for a moment, before realising that the receptionist was watching them with an interest that was way beyond polite. She walked away into the corner and when he didn't immediately follow gave him an impatient come-on beckoning gesture. He sauntered over. The receptionist made a poor attempt not to watch the laconic grace of his movements.

'What do you mean, you didn't make a booking? You had your invitation—where did you think you were going to sleep? On the lawn?'

He shrugged. 'I never got round to booking a room and then, when you asked me to step in as your date, I didn't need to. I'll be staying in your room, won't I?' He put an arm around her shoulders and gave her a squeeze. 'All part of the façade, right?'

She was rendered momentarily speechless by a wave of spicy aftershave and the sudden closeness of him, and then his assumption about their sleeping arrangements slammed into her brain.

'You can't stay in *my* room,' she squeaked.

'The whole weekend takes place at this hotel. It's hardly going to give a loved-up impression if we sneak off to separate rooms at the end of the night, is it?'

'In the Burney family we'd fit right in,' she said, thinking of her parents, who'd had separate bedrooms since she was in her late teens.

He ignored her and turned his head sideways to read the number on the key fob in her hand.

'Eighteen,' he said, heading for the stairs. 'First floor.'

She stumbled after him, her mind reeling. The thought of their sleeping arrangements hadn't entered her head. This was the first time they'd faked their relationship for longer than a couple of hours. She'd simply *assumed* he would have a separate booking.

An image of her vanity case full of embarrassing toiletries danced through her mind, swiftly followed by the fact that her hair looked like a fright wig when she woke up. She gave herself a fast mental slap, because she absolutely did *not* care whether she looked attractive or not, and any attempt to make herself look good was *not* for the benefit of Dan Morgan.

She made a grab for his arm and he turned round on

the landing and looked at her, an expression of amusement on his face.

'I don't see what the problem is,' he said. 'This is a professional arrangement, right? We'll treat it as such. Or were you thinking that I might take advantage of the situation and jump your bones?'

His ice-blue eyes crinkled at the corners as he grinned at her and a flare of heat crept upwards from her neck.

'What am I supposed to think?' she snapped defensively. 'I know what you're like with your five-minute flings. So don't be getting the wrong idea. I am most definitely *not* interested in any shallow no-strings fling. If I'd wanted that I would have stuck with Alistair.'

'I wouldn't *dream* of suggesting one,' he said, holding his hands up. 'The thought never even occurred to me. You're perfectly safe with me.'

Her face burned hotter than ever, because if that wasn't a knock-back she didn't know what was. He was basically telling her she was arrogant for assuming he would *want* to hit on her. Of course he wouldn't. He'd had a year's worth of chances and he'd passed them all up. Her toes curled and she turned away, because her face undoubtedly looked like a tomato right now.

'Look, it's no big deal,' he said. 'We can just shelve the idea. I'll head back to London and you can go it alone.'

A sudden bolt of dread made her stomach lurch as a familiar bugling voice drifted through from Reception.

'Booking for Burney. It'll be one of the higher-end suites—parents of the groom.' A pause. 'The *real* groom, that is…'

Her parents were on the premises and her mother

was obviously on her usual form. Poor Adam. He was relying on her.

She glanced back at Dan. He spread his hands questioningly.

'Your call. Do you need a plus-one or not?'

'This is gorgeous, isn't it?' She sighed as she turned the huge key in the lock and walked ahead of him through the door.

Their cases and bags stood waiting for them at one side of the room, efficiently delivered by the porter. It was everything that a country house hotel bedroom should be. The floorboards were suitably creaky, the dark wood panelling of the walls gleamed, the bed had four posts draped with a soft voile fabric, and there was a pile of squashy pillows and a floral bedspread that matched the silk curtains. Behind a door to one side was a luxurious *en-suite* bathroom.

Dan had to bend slightly to avoid smacking his forehead on the doorjamb. He followed her into the room. She hovered awkwardly by the window, clearly still on edge at the whole room-sharing thing.

'Very nice,' he said and, unable to resist the tease, added, 'Nice, large bed.'

He found his gaze drawn to her face as she dropped her eyes and saw faint colour touch her pale cheekbones. Her obvious awkwardness was seriously cute. His usual dates were pretty full-on—a fast track to the physical. Shyness didn't come into it. It was an odd novelty to be sharing a bedroom with someone without bed actually being on the agenda.

He took pity on her and held his hands up.

'You don't need to worry. I'll take the couch.'

There was a squashy sofa to one side of the window, upholstered in a lavender floral fabric. It would be too short for him, but for a couple of nights it would do.

'We can take it in turns,' she said. 'You take the couch tonight. I'll take it tomorrow.'

Momentarily surprised at the counter-offer, he nodded. Not that he would let her.

'Deal.'

She clapped her hands together and took a business-like breath, as if she were about to start a work meeting.

'Right, then, let's get organised, shall we? This can be my space…' she moved one of the smaller pieces of her vast luggage collection onto a dark wood bureau with an ornate mirror '…and this can be yours.' She waved a hand at the antique desk. 'You get the desk and com-plimentary Wi-Fi. Should be right up your street. I can't imagine you needing much else.'

'You make me sound like some workaholic.'

'I hate to break it to you…' she said, nodding at his minimal luggage, which included a laptop bag. 'It's hardly a get-away-from-it-all minibreak, is it? You've brought your office with you!'

'Only out of habit,' he protested. 'I take the laptop everywhere. Doesn't mean I'm going to use it.'

She turned back to him and pulled a sceptical face. He held his hands up.

'And somewhere in here…' she shuffled through the wad of check-in bumph '…is the itinerary for the week-end. Might as well know what we're up against. Blimey, we'll hardly have time to draw breath.'

He took it from her—a piece of stiff white card dec-orated in eye-watering yellow. He was suddenly very aware as he looked at the packed agenda that he would be joined at the hip with her pretty much twenty-four-seven for the next couple of days—a situation he hadn't really considered properly when he'd made light of the room-sharing thing.

It all seemed a bit less amusing now they were actually in the room and she was talking him through their shared personal space and unpacking what seemed like endless belongings. He avoided guests at his flat as much as possible. One night was his limit, with sex the sole item on the agenda. Conversation and space-sharing didn't come into it. He simply didn't *do* the give and take required to cohabit. Not any more. He'd done it once and he had no inclination to be reminded of the lash-up he'd made of it.

Just a weekend. He latched on to that thought.

'Certainly not doing a small quickie wedding, are they?' he commented, speed-reading the itinerary.

Emma leaned in close to look at the card with him and he picked up a soft, sweet wave of the scent she always wore as she tucked a stray lock of hair behind her ear. His pulse stepped up a notch in response.

He wasn't used to her looking dressed down like this. That was all it was. Their usual encounters involved smart, polished business dress or the occasional evening gown for gala dinners and the like. Even then her outfits were always reserved, and he couldn't remember a time when he'd seen her in jeans or when she'd worn her hair down. Now it fell softly to her shoulders in waves, framing her heart-shaped face. When you took the time to look behind her uptight attitude, she was actually very pretty.

'When has Adam ever done anything on a small scale?' she said. 'It just wouldn't be him, would it?'

He refocused his attention on the itinerary.

'So, this evening there's welcome drinks on the terrace. Then tomorrow the wedding is here in the grounds, followed by a night of celebration. And then a slap-up cooked breakfast the morning after. That marquee must be for the wedding.' He nodded out of the window.

She followed his gaze, then moved away and sat down on the edge of the bed.

'Adam must be mad,' she said. She bounced up and down on the mattress approvingly.

Dan leaned against one of the posts at the foot of the bed, watching her. Diaphanous fabric softly draped over it—white with a tiny pale yellow flower print.

'Why? Because his wedding's the size of an elephant or just because there *is* a wedding?' he said.

She looked up at him, a tiny smile touching the corner of her lush mouth, and he had a sudden image of himself leaning her slowly back onto the floral quilt and finding out what she tasted like.

He stood up straight and gave himself a mental shake. What the hell was he thinking? This was a last-ditch platonic date—not one of his conquests. The fact that the venue involved a bedroom instead of a boardroom didn't change the fact that their relationship was work-based. It also didn't seem to stop the slow burn that had kicked in low in his abdomen.

'Both,' she said, and shrugged.

'Is that because of Alistair? I mean, you've got to admit he was a bit of a curveball. You *never* date. Not in all the time I've known you. And then suddenly in the space of a few weeks you're packing up and leaving.'

She didn't answer for a moment. There was a distant expression on her face, as if she was thinking it over.

'Partly because of Alistair,' she said at last. 'But really what happened with him was probably inevitable. Meeting the right person isn't something I've excelled at so far. He was so attentive and considerate that I thought for once I'd really cracked it. I really believed it was something special. But it was the same old story.'

She smiled at him, an I-don't-care smile that was just a bit too small to be convincing, and he felt a sudden spike of dislike for Alistair.

'Same old story?'

She sighed. 'Maybe you had a point when you said I was a bit star-struck—I don't know,' she said, picking at a loose thread on the floral quilt.

There was an air of defeat about her that made him want to kick Alistair's butt.

'I got a bit swept up in all the excitement of it. It wasn't so much him as the idea of *life* with him. It was exciting. It was glamorous. It was everything that I'm not.'

'It was two-dimensional Hollywood claptrap. Who wants to live in a shallow world like that? You can't be the first person to get sucked in, but you're the most grounded person I know. You'll soon get over that cardboard idiot.'

That made her smile, lighting her face. He liked her looking happy like that. He liked that he'd *caused* her to look like that.

'I won't be making the same mistake again,' she said. 'I'm going to put *myself* first from now on. But even if one day I do find the right person I won't be getting married with my parents in tow. *No way.* Nice plane trip to a beach somewhere with a couple of random witnesses.'

He grinned.

'What about you?' she said, wiping the smile right off his face.

'What *about* me?'

'Come on—surprise me. What kind of wedding would you have if you could choose?' She leaned back on her palms and narrowed her eyes at him. 'Some beach thing in the Maldives?' She flapped a hand. 'No, no, let me guess… It would be something small. You could probably do it in a lunch hour if you wanted to—take an hour or so out and nip to the registry office. Quick glass of champagne, handful of confetti, and then you could get back to work.'

'Very funny.'

Terrific. He should have seen that coming. The last thing he needed right now was a chat about marriage aspirations. He just wanted to get through this weekend and get on with his life. And he didn't even have his own hotel room to retreat to.

He moved away from the bed to look out of the window, his back to her.

'Of course you'd have to stick at a relationship for longer than a month, then, wouldn't you?' she teased.

He didn't look round. 'It has nothing to do with sticking at a relationship. I have to prioritise. The business is growing at a massive rate. I need to put all my energy into that.'

'Nobody needs to work twenty-four-seven,' she said. 'Not even you. Maybe you should think about slowing down, or at least taking a breather. I just don't get why you're so crazy for work. I've never known anyone so obsessed. And it's not like you've got anyone to share the rewards with. None of your girls last five minutes.'

He stared across the hotel lawn at the dense woodland right in the distance on the skyline. Stared at it but didn't see it.

Another image flashed through his mind in its place. *Sticking at relationships. Sharing the rewards. Maggie.* Dark-haired Maggie with her gentle smile and her kindness.

Maggie and—

He stamped hard and fast on that thought before it could multiply. What the hell was his stupid brain doing, dragging that old stuff up?

At the faint sound of voices and car doors slamming he glanced down onto the gravel drive as Adam emerged, beaming, from a yellow Rolls-Royce, quiff cemented in place, wearing dark glasses like a celebrity. Ernie was right by his side. A gang of porters staggered under a stack of luggage. Obviously overpacking ran in the family.

'Your brother's here,' he said, to distract her, because he couldn't imagine a time when he'd be keen to discuss his future wedding plans.

Emma scrambled off the bed and joined Dan at the window.

'We'd better get ready for the drinks party,' she said, turning to her heap of luggage and proceeding to unzip.

He checked his watch.

'But it's *hours* away.'

As if that mattered…

'I need to make a good impression,' she said. 'I hate being late. And you have to help me keep my parents in check.'

She looked up at him, suddenly feeling awkward,

with a bottle of pink shower gel in one hand and a loofah in the other.

'Do you want to use the bathroom first? I mean, perhaps we should work out some kind of rota.'

'For Pete's sake, we don't need a rota,' he said, his tone exasperated. 'It's two days. You take the bathroom first. You're bound to take longer.'

'What's that supposed to mean?' She made an indignant face. 'That you look great just the way you are but I'm some hag who needs work?'

He laughed out loud.

'No. It means I've never met a woman who takes less than half an hour to get ready.'

She turned towards the bathroom, her arms now full of toiletries.

'And you don't look like a hag,' he called after her. 'You never have.'

It was the nearest thing to a compliment he'd ever given her.

CHAPTER FIVE

DAN GAZED OUT of the open hotel room window and listened to the soft sound of falling water from the shower in the *en-suite* bathroom. It had kicked in five minutes after Emma had shut the door firmly and twisted the lock, as if she thought he might burst in on her.

The marquee was now bathed in early-evening golden sunshine. The sweeping lawns were perfectly manicured, and a lily pond lay on the far right of his view. If he leaned forward far enough he could see an ornate wrought-iron bench set to one side of it. He wondered how many brides' backsides had been plonked there over the years. It really was the perfect photo opportunity.

He was at the cream of wedding venues in the south of England and it was only natural that it might whip up a few passing thoughts of his one and only brush with marriage, right? Just fleeting thoughts… That was all.

Maggie and Blob.

The name filtered back into his mind before he could stop it.

Blob, he had called him—or her—after the fuzzy early scan which had been completely unintelligible to both of them except for the blob with the strong and speedy heartbeat. It had made Maggie laugh. An interim holding name while they bandied about proper full-on names. Andy or Emily. Sam or Molly. To delete as appropriate once they knew the gender, at a later date that had never arrived.

Four months hadn't been later enough.

Maggie and Blob.

An unexpected twist of long-suppressed dull pain flared in his chest—the blunt ache of an old injury. He wrenched his mind away forcibly. For Pete's sake, what was he *doing*? He did *not* need a pointless trip down memory lane right now.

He rationalised madly. He hadn't been near a wedding in donkey's years. Without a family to speak of, things like weddings didn't crop up all that often, and this place was Wedding Central. It was bound to stir things up. But that was all this was—just a momentary blip. He had dealt with Maggie and Blob. They were part of the past and he'd left them there with admirable efficiency. He'd dealt with it all and moved on.

Perhaps that was part of the problem. His life was drifting into predictability, leaving his mind free to wander where it shouldn't be going. He needed to up the stakes at work—perhaps a new business venture. Work had always been the solution before.

The shower splashed on and on, and judging by the enormous bag of toiletries Emma had heaved in there with her she wasn't going to be emerging any time soon. There was no time like the present when it came to refocusing your mind. He unzipped his laptop bag and sat down at the antique desk.

Emma gave her reflection one last glance in the steamy-edged mirror and paused to let her heart reconsider its decision to take a sprint. She knew she'd spent far too long rubbing in scented body lotion and blitzing body hair, telling herself it was because she wanted to make a good impression on Ernie's family. For Adam. It had absolutely nothing to do with the fact that Dan was on the other side of that door. He was fully rationalised. Whatever there was between them, it would always have terms. It would always be about work.

But he could easily have refused to accompany her here. I mean, really, what was in it for him? She knew she'd annoyed him with the public break-up thing, but he had no real understanding of how things were with her parents—how the pursuit of an easy life had become the norm for her. It was her defence mechanism against the endless nagging, and that was what Dan had been. Her route to an easy life. Shame it had all been fictional.

But still he was here.

And now there was that tiny nagging voice, whispering that he might just have come to his senses since she'd broken the news that she was leaving. He might have suddenly realised she meant more to him than a handy work date. Could that be why he now *wanted* the arrangement to end, despite his reluctance to let it go at first? Perhaps this weekend could lead to something more than a platonic agreement between them.

It was a *stupid* nagging voice. To listen to it, or even worse to act on it, would be to set herself up for humiliation. Was the Alistair debacle not enough evidence that she had warped judgement when it came to decoding male behaviour?

The twisty lurch of disappointment in her stomach when she opened the bathroom door told her she'd been stupid to read anything into his presence here.

He was still wearing the same jeans and T-shirt, he'd clearly made zero effort to unpack his minimal luggage, and worst of all he was leaning into his laptop where it stood open on the desk, surrounded by the usual scattering of work papers.

Had she actually thought for a moment that his presence here might have anything to do with an increased regard for her? What a fool she was. Nothing had changed between them at all. She was imagining the whole damn thing just because he'd shown her some support. Clearly she was desperate for attention now Alistair had humiliated her.

At best, Dan wanted to part on good terms—*that* was why he'd decided to accompany her to the wedding and help her out this last time. There was nothing more to it than that.

Undoubtedly the fact that the hotel had complimentary Wi-Fi had made the decision a whole lot easier for him.

Dan stared at her as she stood in the doorway, the deliciously sensual scent of her body lotion mingling with steam, epically failing to register the look of resigned disapproval on her face because of her transformation from office starch.

Her dark hair fell in damp tendrils, framing her heart-shaped face, and there was a pink hue to her usually pale skin. She was totally swamped by one of the enormous white his 'n' hers hotel bathrobes, and his mind immediately insisted on debating what she might or might not be wearing underneath.

He stared hard at the e-mail on his computer screen until his eyes watered, in the hope that his stupid body would realise that they might be sharing a bedroom and a bathroom but their interaction was limited to the professional—just the way it always was. For the third time he read it without taking a single word in.

'You're working,' she said with ill-hidden disappointment. 'Don't you ever take a break?'

He felt a surge of exasperation.

'What else was I meant to do? Take a stroll round the grounds? Sit and watch the bathroom door? It's just a couple of e-mails while I waited for you to be finished.'

'Well, there's no need to snap,' she said, crossing the room to the bureau and squeezing a handful of her hair with the corner of a towel. 'You could have gone first if you'd wanted to.'

Oh, for Pete's sake! He hadn't counted on the inconvenient need to be constantly polite that their space-sharing had caused. Without the shared goal of sleeping together it boiled down to a *you-go-first-no-you-I-insist* awkwardness about using the facilities.

With a monumental effort he curbed his irritation.

'I'm sorry,' he said. 'I'm just not really used to sharing my personal space, that's all. I'm used to doing what I like whenever I want to.'

She glanced at him and smiled.

'That's OK.'

She began combing her long hair out, looking at her reflection in the mirror.

'You have a different girlfriend every week,' she said. 'I'd have thought bedroom etiquette was your speciality.'

He watched as she sprayed perfume on her neck and pulse points. The intense scent of it made his senses reel.

'That's different.'

'I don't see how.'

He shrugged.

'There's no give and take needed. They stay over and the next morning they leave. There's no personal belongings cluttering up every surface.' He glanced at the bed, currently festooned with her clothes. 'There's no pussyfooting around each other over who's hogging the bathroom. It's done and dusted, with minimal disruption.'

And minimal emotional input. Which was exactly how he liked it.

'You make it sound *so* romantic,' she said sarcastically, dipping her finger in a pot of pink make-up and dabbing it gently over her mouth.

His eyes seemed to be glued to the tiny movements and to the delicious pink sheen it gave her luscious lower lip. She didn't notice, focusing on what she was doing in the mirror.

'It isn't *meant* to be romantic,' he said. 'It is what it is.'

A temporary and very enjoyable diversion, with no lasting repercussions.

'So it's fine for them to stay over until you get what you want, and then they're ejected from the premises at breakfast time? Is that it?'

'You make it sound callous,' he said, snapping his laptop shut and gathering up his work papers. 'When actually it's fun.' She threw him a sceptical glance and he couldn't resist adding, 'Hot, steamy, no-holds-barred fun,' just to see if he could make her blush again.

'You have no scruples,' she complained.

He saw the flush of pink creep softly along her cheekbones, highlighting them prettily. Sparring with her was actually turning out to be enjoyable.

'I don't need scruples,' he said. 'We're all adults. I never make any promises that I don't keep. I'm honest with them about not wanting anything serious and they appreciate that.'

'No, they don't,' she said. 'They might say they're fine with it, but in reality they're hoping it will turn into more. It's not the same for women. Sleeping with someone isn't some throwaway thing. It's a big deal—an emotional investment. And, anyway, if you always put those limits in place when you meet someone you're cutting out the chance of ever having a proper relationship. You could meet the perfect person for you and she'd just slip through your fingers unnoticed.' She fluttered her fingers in the air to press her point. 'You'd never even know. You'll be perpetually single.'

'And that,' he said, grabbing his bag and making for the bathroom, 'is exactly the point.'

He smiled at the roll of her eyes as he closed the door.

Emma didn't usually go in for a second coat of mascara. Or a second squirt of perfume just to make sure it lasted the distance. But then she didn't usually go in for room-sharing. She wished someone would tell her stupid pulse rate that it was supposed to be platonic.

He had the speediest bathroom habits she'd ever come across, and as a result she was still balancing on one leg, one foot in her knickers and the other out, when the lock clicked and the bathroom door opened. Heart thundering, she thanked her lucky stars that she'd decided to keep the bathrobe on while dressing, and covered her fluster by whipping her panties on at breakneck speed, clamping the robe around her and then giving him a manic grin that probably bordered on cheesy.

Her entire consciousness immediately zeroed in on the fact that he had a fluffy white towel wrapped around his muscular hips and absolutely nothing else. The faint hint of a tan highlighted his broad chest and the most defined set of abs she'd ever seen outside a magazine. He rubbed a second towel over his hair, spiking it even beyond the usual.

She forced her eyes away, snatched the bathrobe more tightly around her and crossed to the bed.

'I think we should have a quick round-up of the ground rules for tonight,' she said, flipping through some of the clothes laid out on the bed, not really seeing them, just aiming to look busy.

'Did you just say "ground rules"?'

She glanced up and had to consciously drag her eyes upwards from his drum-tight torso. His amused grin told her that unfortunately he'd clocked her doing it, so she pressed the platonic angle hard to show him that they might be sharing a hotel room but she had no romantic interest in him whatsoever. None. Zilch.

'I did. We need to pull off being the perfect couple.'

He let out an amused breath. 'I think you can count on *me* to know how to do that,' he said.

She silently marvelled. He obviously thought a few posh dinners and hot sex was all it took.

'This is a whole different ball game. When you've been my date before it's mostly been an hour or two alone with my family in a restaurant. A trained chimp could probably pull that off. This is going to be a lot more full-on. The place is going to be stuffed with Ernie's family. We need to make a good impression for Adam. We have to look totally together but in an *über*-normal way, so we can counteract my parents' dysfunctional relationship.'

He looked briefly skyward. One hand rested on the

desk; the other was caught in his hair. By sheer will she didn't look at the towel, held up only by a single fold. Instead she fixed her eyes on his face.

'You're over-analysing,' he said. 'Trust me on this.'

He pulled a few items from his bag and headed back to the bathroom with them slung over his arm.

'I know how to pull off loved-up,' he called over his shoulder, with not a hint of trepidation at the evening ahead when *she* was a bag of nerves. 'Just like you know how to pull off professional couple. Just leave it to me.'

A couple of hours' work had certainly done the trick in terms of refocusing him. He'd fired off a ton of important e-mails, had a look through some figures, and if he needed any more of a distraction to stop his mind dredging up the past, looking at Emma as he emerged from the bathroom again was it.

Fully dressed now, she was wearing her hair long again, this time brushed to one side, so it lay gleaming over one shoulder of the soft green maxi-dress she wore. Her newly applied perfume made his pulse jump and she wore more make-up than usual, highlighting her wide brown eyes and the delectable softness of her lips.

Playing the part of boyfriend to *that* for the evening was hardly going to be a chore.

He could tell she was nervous just by the way she was behaving. Give her a room full of professionals and she could network her way around it with the best of them, holding her own no matter who he introduced her to. But with the prospect of a weekend with her own family she was reduced to a quivering shadow of her work self.

That very jumpiness seemed to heighten his awareness of her on some level, and it felt perfectly natural for him to lean in close to her on the way down the passage towards the stairs. He rested his hand lightly around her waist, conscious of her slenderness beneath the light flowing drape of her dress.

Emma was hotly aware of him next to her as he escorted her along the landing. As his arm curled around her waist she picked up the spicy scent of his aftershave on warm skin and her stomach gave a slow and far too delicious flip. Everything about him seemed to be overstepping the lines of her personal space in a way it never had before. The way he stood just a fraction closer to her than strictly necessary… The way he'd held her gaze a beat too long when he'd teased her about wanting ground rules.

'Er…there's no one actually here to see us,' she pointed out, glancing down at his hand, now resting softly on her hip. She looked up at him questioningly.

'Just getting into character,' he said easily, not moving his hand.

'I'm determined to inject a bit of tradition if it kills me, Donald,' she heard suddenly.

Her mother's distinctive tones drifted down the corridor from behind them and she froze next to Dan. And then they were getting louder.

'I think I'll have a word with Ernie's parents about top tables and speeches. It's a family occasion. They'll be expecting us to have some input.'

Emma's heart began to sink at the thought of her mother instigating a cosy chat about traditional wedding roles with Ernie's clearly far more liberal parents and she stopped at the top of the stairs, intending to intercept her and suggest a new approach of just enjoying the celebrations without actually *criticising* any of them.

The coherence of that thought dissolved into nothing as Dan suddenly curled his hand tighter around her waist and propelled her back against the nearest wall. Before she could so much as let out a squeak, he kissed her.

CHAPTER SIX

NIGH ON EIGHT months of conditioning herself that her attraction to him was just a stupid crush, and all it took to get every nerve-ending of attraction right back in action was one kiss. One kiss that made her toes curl and her stomach feel as if it might have turned into warm marshmallow.

He caught her lower lip perfectly between his own lips and sucked gently on it, his hand sliding lower to cup the curve of her bottom. The smooth wood panelling of the wall pressed against her back. She could feel every hard, muscular contour of his body against hers, and sparks danced down her spine and pooled deliciously between her legs.

Her eyes fluttered dreamily shut—and when she opened them she was staring right into the disapproving gaze of her mother, a vision in purple sequins, a few feet away over Dan's shoulder.

Reality clattered over her like a bucket of ice cubes and she wriggled away from him, the flat of her hand against the hardness of his chest, her heart racing. He made no effort to disengage whatsoever, so she added an extra pace's worth of space between them herself.

He was watching her steadily, the petrol-blue shirt he

was wearing making his eyes seem darker than usual, a grin playing about his lips. Her heart raced as if she'd just sprinted up and down the creaky stairs a few dozen times.

She tore her gaze away from his.

'Mum!' she gabbled.

'Hello, darling.' Her father leaned in to give her a kiss and shook Dan's hand.

Her mother glanced at him disapprovingly.

'Really, Emma,' she remarked. 'A little class would be good. *Anyone* could walk along this corridor and how do you think it would look to find you two in a clinch?' She radiated criticism, despite the fact that she was intending to steam in and openly re-evaluate the wedding plans. When it came to social etiquette she could be remarkably selective. 'You're not sixteen, you know. A little decorum would be good. Thank goodness Adam can rely on your father and me to make a good impression.'

She swept past them down the stairs.

Emma stared after her incredulously and then rounded on Dan.

'What the hell was that about?' she snapped. 'What did you think you were *doing?*'

'We've got an image to keep up,' he said, shrugging as if he'd done nothing wrong.

So he'd just been playing a part, while her knees had turned to jelly. There had been a moment back there when she'd thought she might simply fold into a hot puddle on the floor.

But he didn't need to know that, did he?

'I don't think we need to take things quite *that* far,' she said, trying to breathe normally.

'Are you complaining that my kisses are somehow

substandard?' he said, his gaze penetrating, a grin touching the edge of his mouth and crinkling his eyes.

Her blush felt as if it spread all the way from the roots of her hair to her toes, because as kisses went it had been utterly off-the-scale sublime.

'Of course I'm not saying that,' she snapped. 'It's just that when I said we were aiming for perfect couple I obviously should have specified that I didn't mean perfect couple at honeymoon stage.'

'What *were* you aiming for, then?' he said, blue eyes amused. He rubbed his lips thoughtfully with his fingers, as if he was savouring the taste of her.

She ran a hand self-consciously over her hair. Perhaps if she could smooth the muss out of it she could smooth the fluster out of the rest of her.

'I was thinking more comfortable in each other's company. You know the kind of thing. More the on-the-brink-of-settling-down stage.' She shrugged, her pulse returning to normal now. 'Then again, you're clearly drawing on your own experiences. When did you last have a relationship that made it past loved-up? You go from meet straight to dump. You miss out everything in between.'

He laughed, clearly amused by the whole affair.

'You gave it one hundred and ten per cent when you were staging our "break-up",' he pointed out, making sarcastic speech marks in the air with his fingers. 'Right the way down to the spectacular drink-throwing. What's the matter with that approach now?'

She could hardly say it made her knees unreliable, could she?

'Because the whole point of this is to stop my parents showing Adam up,' she said. 'And they've actually as good as just told *us* to get a room. I think we might have taken it a *teensy* bit too far.'

She led the way down the stairs

'Spoilsport,' he called after her, kick-starting her blush all over again.

As they walked out through wide-open double doors onto a stone-flagged terrace she was more aware than ever of his hand pressed softly in the hollow of her back. It seemed to generate sparks of heat that climbed tantalisingly up her spine. Her mind insisted on re-playing his kiss on a loop, making her feel completely flustered.

Fortunately she had the reality check of Adam's flamboyant styling to smack her between the eyes. The terrace was softly lit by hurricane lamps on tables and pin-lights strung along the stone balustrade. A band were set up to one side, playing jaunty music to which none of the guests were dancing because they were all crowded around the centrepiece in the middle of the terrace.

For a moment she had to lean back and narrow her eyes while her brain processed exactly what it was.

Adam and Ernie had apparently commissioned a life-size ice sculpture of themselves. It gleamed in the floor-level spotlighting. It depicted Adam with one finger pressed against his temple in a thoughtful pose while Ernie looked on.

Her parents were standing to one side, and her mother's face was a stunned picture. On the bright side, at least it appeared to have rendered her speechless. As soon as she saw Emma and Dan she crossed to them, the beads on her purple evening dress shimmering as she walked. She wouldn't have looked out of place in a ballroom dance show.

The real Adam and Ernie joined them, wearing complementary head-to-toe designer suits, with a group of Ernie's relatives flanking them.

'Aren't they *fabulous?*' Adam was gushing, clasping his hands together in delight. 'And the best thing about having yourself carved is that you can tweak the way you look. So I made myself taller and we had a bit shaved off Ernie's nose.'

'Well, I've got to be honest, I'm not that impressed,' her mother sniffed, deploying her usual tactic: if it was outside her comfort zone then she was suspicious of it. She leaned backwards appraisingly. 'They've made your ears stick out,' she remarked to Adam. 'How much did you pay for them?'

'Mum, you can't ask things like that,' Emma said, smiling nervously at the group.

Her mother drew herself up to her full height and pursed her lips. 'Of course I can. Adam's my son. We're parents of the groom. I'm entitled to my opinion.'

'They were a gift,' Adam said, pink-cheeked. 'From Ernie's aunt. She's a sculptress. She spent *hours* working on them. In a freezer.'

There was an ensuing pin-drop silence, during which Emma's father took a canapé from a passing waiter and attempted to lever it into his mouth.

'No more of those tartlets, Donald,' her mother said, leaning in as if with a sixth sense. She expertly took the canapé out of his hand and his teeth closed over thin air. 'Cholesterol!' she snapped.

Ernie dragged a blushing Adam away to circulate, and Emma did her best to stand in as sounding board for her

mother's stream-of-consciousness opinions on every mi-
nuscule aspect of the proceedings. She was vaguely and
gratefully aware of Dan's calming presence at her side.

How would she manage at things like this in future,
without him watching her back? The thought of losing
that comfort gave her a needling sense of dread.

A couple of hours later she was worn out with smiling and small talk and her mother seemed to have re-
connected with a kindred spirit in the shape of Emma's
spinster aunt Mabel, last seen at a childhood Christmas
before moving up north. Emma watched them across the
terrace, their arms folded in matching poses, matching
critical expressions on their faces. Although her voice
was drowned out by the music, she saw her mother's
lips form the word *grandchildren* as the pair of them
looked her way.

She turned to see her father surreptitiously sliding
food from the buffet table onto an already heaped plate
while her mother was preoccupied.

'Your mother's got me on a diet,' he said when he saw
her disbelieving stare.

'Doesn't sound like much fun,' Dan said.

He shrugged.

'It's not so bad. I have a second lunch down at the golf
club most days. They do a fantastic pie and crinkle-cut
chips. What she doesn't know, and all that.'

Oh, for Pete's sake, she'd had just about enough of
this.

'I need a walk,' she said, heading for the steps down
from the terrace and onto the lawns.

'I'll come with you.'

Dan followed her away from the party, grabbing a
couple of champagne flutes from a passing waiter.

* * *

It was a beautiful clear summer night, the velvety cropped lawn silver in the moonlight. Strings of pearly pin-lights lent the trees a fairy-tale quality.

Emma walked on her toes at first, to stop her three-inch heels sinking into the grass, then gave up and took them off, walking barefoot, with the hem of her dress sweeping the grass. Dan was acutely aware of the change in their height difference. Now she seemed small and fragile as she walked next to him.

The faint sound of music and laughter drifted after them on the night air as the party carried on up on the terrace. The lawn swept gently downwards towards a small lake, molten metal in the moonlight. The fresh, sweet scent of dewy grass hung on the cool night air.

'And you wonder why marriage doesn't appeal to me,' she said as he fell into step beside her. 'If I ever found the right man why the hell would I marry him, if that's what it does to you? They lead separate lives. Separate rooms, separate friends. He spends his life trying to exist below her radar and she's got zero excitement in her own life so she makes up for it with gossip and by meddling in Adam's life and in mine. And yet they think they're presenting the image of joint marital solidarity.'

She warmed to her subject, flinging up an exasperated hand.

'Is that how I'll end up if I have kids? With them arguing over who *isn't* going to have the annoying old cow over at Christmas?'

He couldn't keep in a grin. She was so indignant.

'It's not all bad,' he said. 'At least they *are* interested in you.'

She sighed.

'On an interfering kind of a level, maybe.'

He shook his head.

'Maybe it comes across like that. OK, OK—it *does* come across like that,' he said as she gave him an incredulous look. 'But still you're lucky to be part of a family. I couldn't believe it when you said you were thinking about throwing it all away for some guy you'd known five minutes.'

Emma hid her fluster at his unexpected mention of Alistair by zeroing in on his other point. *Family* and *Dan* weren't really two words she thought of in the same sentence.

'That was part of the attraction,' she said. 'The idea of having some fun, for a change, with someone who put me first without criticising, without comparing me—who put me ahead of everything else. And with Alistair there was no prospect of settling into anything like my parents' take on domesticity. It would have been loads of travel and excitement, minimal chance of ending up in separate bedrooms living my life through my kids.'

'So the whole thing with Alistair was about you proving a point to your family? Why does it bother you so much what they think?'

Dan's comment made her feel as if she was being sloshed with cold water—especially as it was so astute. She *had* been blinded to Alistair by the desire to impress her parents.

'It had nothing to do with proving a point,' she lied. 'I'm a grown-up. What bothered me when I was a kid is just an exasperation now.'

She stopped to sit down on the bench he'd seen earlier from the bedroom window. He sat down next to her, the hard wrought-iron pressing cold through his shirt. He handed her one of the champagne flutes.

'Then what is it?' he said. 'You handle yourself brilliantly back in London. You're a real slick professional. You don't need to let anyone's criticism bother you.'

She stared across the silvery lawn. Faint laughter drifted across from the terrace.

'Ah, but that's exactly the point,' she said. 'When we see each other it's usually for some work reason or other. When it comes to work I know I can hold my own. I know what I'm talking about. I make sure I won't get caught out or make a slip-up.' She paused. 'It hasn't always been like that for me.'

'So what *was* it like, then?'

Emma looked at him, trying to gauge whether his interest was real or counterfeit. He'd never shown an interest in finding out more about her before—not unless it was related to work, of course. His blue eyes held hers steadily. She took a sip of her drink and smiled a little, remembering, letting the years fall away.

'Growing up, I was the clumsiest kid you can imagine,' she said. 'If anyone was going to make a fool of herself it was me. And it was even more difficult because Adam's always been such an overachiever. I started out at school trying to work hard, but it never seemed to matter how much effort I put in. I was never quite good enough to earn Adam's level of interest or praise. He was picking up A grades, winning competitions, excelling at everything. After a while I learned not to put myself in a position where people could notice I was falling short.'

A memory returned to her in all its cringeworthy glory. 'I had a part in the school musical once.' She looked up at him. 'When I was thirteen. Can you imagine me doing that?'

He shrugged, a small smile on his face. A polite response.

'They used to do a musical every year. It was so popular. Everyone would come and watch—parents, locals. And that year they were doing *Grease*. Loads of singing and dancing. I was so excited by the whole idea. I just wanted to be part of it. It didn't occur to me that there could be a negative side, that things could go wrong. I was so naïve.'

'What happened?'

She put her head in her hands and pulled a cringing face.

'I forgot my lines. I stood on that stage and looked out at the hall, knowing it was packed, and I couldn't remember a word. And I don't mean I stumbled over my lines. I didn't just have a bit of a blip and then pick things up. My mind went completely blank. I froze. The lights were bright in my face, but I could still see the shadows of all the people. The music was so loud I could hardly think.'

'What did you do?'

'I ran off the stage and refused to go back on. They put the understudy on instead. My parents were in the audience and my mother gave me hell. She still brings it up now and then. I think in some part of her mind I'm still that nervy thirteen-year-old who had a public meltdown onstage and showed her up.'

She took a sip of her champagne, thinking back. The bright lights in her eyes. The cold horror rushing through her as she tried and failed to make her panicked brain work. The slick of sweat on her palms.

She looked across at Dan, easily pasting a smile on

her face. She'd had years of practice at doing it. She was an adult now, with her own life, and she didn't need to be defined by that awful feeling of failure—not any more. Yet on some level maybe it could never be erased.

'That's awful.'

She shrugged, smiling a little.

'It was at the time. I was mortified. And it never happened again—not to that extent. I never put myself out there again after that—not in any situation where I couldn't trust myself to get it right. I concentrated on academic stuff instead of the arts. Left all that to Adam. And, well, you can see how good *he* was at it. That's partly why I decided to study law. A lot of it is about bulk learning. If you know the rules you can apply them. If you put the work in you can build a career. It isn't left to the whim of anyone else liking what you do in order to secure your success.'

He watched her, looking down at her hands, her skin silvery pale in the moonlight, contrasting with her gleaming dark hair. The air of vulnerability about her made his heart turn over softly. He had an unexpected urge to sweep her into his arms and erase all that self-doubt, make her feel special.

'You care far too much what people think of you,' he said.

She frowned.

'Isn't that what everyone wants, though? Validation from everyone else? Or at least from the people you care about.'

'Maybe. But sometimes love doesn't show up as hugs and presents,' he said. 'Not everything is that in-your-face in life. Your mum, for example, shows she cares by—'

'By being the most interfering woman on the planet?

Maybe. But just a little…' she searched for the right word '…*positivity* might be nice now and then.'

She leaned back a little, surveying him with interest.

'I didn't think you had such strong feelings about family,' she said. 'It's not like I see you jumping through any hoops to see yours. You never seem to visit them— you never even mention them. They can't be any more of a nightmare than mine are, and even I do my duty and see them every few months.'

'Why?'

'What do you mean, *why?*'

'Why do you do your duty and see them? It's perfectly clear you don't relish spending time with them. Why don't you just cut them out of your life if they're that much of a chore?'

He made a slicing motion with his hand while she stared at him, momentarily speechless.

'I couldn't do that,' she said at last. 'They're my family.'

'You mean you care about them?'

'Of course I do. I've kind of got used to the criticism in a way. It's who they are. They might be a nightmare, but at least they're mine.'

'And there's your answer.'

She shook her head faintly at him.

'To what?'

'You were wondering why I never mention or see my family. There's your answer. That's the difference between you and me. I don't really have a family—not as such. And what I did have of one was never remotely interested in me, even in a critical way.'

She dropped her eyes from his.

'Look, I'm sorry…' she began.

He smiled at her.

'Don't be. I'm fine with it. It's always been that way. I don't *need* a family, Emma. What you don't have you don't miss. When I was a kid we didn't do overbearing parents or criticism or sibling rivalry.' He paused. 'We didn't actually *do* family.'

His mind waved the memory of Maggie before him again with a flourish and he clenched his teeth hard. Talking about family with Emma wasn't so difficult when it related to his mother. His feelings for her had progressed over the years to end up somewhere near contempt. But family as related to Maggie meant something completely different. That had been his hope. That had been their plan. Losing that planned future had somehow been so much worse than losing any excuse for a family he might have had in the past.

She was staring at him. He could feel it. He stood up, began walking back to the terrace, deliberately not looking at her.

'What do you mean, you didn't do family?' she said, catching him up, her long skirt caught in one hand.

He thought fleetingly about simply closing the conversation down, but found that on some level he didn't want to. When had he last talked his childhood over with anyone? His usual conquests were happy to go along with however much he told them about himself—or, more to the point, however little. There had never been any need to give much away. Dinner and a cocktail or two seemed to be all that was needed to get to first base, quickly followed by second and third.

'Exactly that,' he said. 'My upbringing wasn't in a nice suburban house with a mum and dad, siblings, pets. Out of all those things some of the time I had a mum.'

'What about your dad?'

'I've never known him.'

The look of sympathy on her face was immediate and he instantly brushed it away with a wave of his hand.

'I've never needed to know him. It's no big deal.'

It was a billion times easier to talk about the family he'd actually had than the one he'd wanted and lost. The two things were worlds apart in his mind.

'Yes, it is. That's awful.'

He shrugged.

'What about your mum, then? You must have been close if it was just the two of you.'

He could feel his lip trying to give a cynical curl.

'Not especially. She wasn't exactly Mother of the Year.' He caught sight of her wide-eyed look and qualified resignedly, 'Oh, hell, she was very young. It can't have been easy, raising a kid by herself. It just was what it was.'

Maggie flashed through his mind again. They'd been young, too, and totally unprepared for parenthood. But walking away had never been an option for him. He'd known that from the very first moment she'd told him about her pregnancy.

'She worked on and off,' he said. 'Bar work, mostly. When I was smaller I used to stay with a neighbour, or one or other of her friends. There was never any consistency to it. Then when I got older it was just me.'

He paused for a second, because that couple of sentences didn't really sum up what it had felt like in that house by himself. It had been cold, with a musty smell of damp that had never gone away, even in the summer. Never tidy. Ready meals and late-night movies because no one cared if he stayed up late or if he was getting enough sleep for school. Sometimes his mother had stayed out all night until he'd wondered if she'd return at all. What would happen to him then? Where would he go? The uncertainty of it all had made him constantly on edge.

'I'd never have known,' she said. 'You've done so well to get out from under all that.'

Emma felt a sudden stab of shame at her fussing about her own childhood. She must sound like some dreadful attention-seeker to him, with her comfortable middle-class upbringing, moaning that she'd never seemed able to please her family when he'd barely had one.

'Not especially. I think it did me a favour. I was so determined to find a way out of there, and when I went to college I found it. Not long after that I had the idea for my first business. It was a coffee kiosk. The cafeteria on campus really sucked. It was poorly run, and there was no facility for grabbing a coffee on the go. So I plugged the gap. It wasn't much more than a trolley at first, but I could see what worked and what didn't. I developed the business, ran it during my free periods, and pretty soon I was making good money. And that was when I *really* knew.'

'Knew what?'

He glanced across at her then, and the look in his eyes was intense in the moonlight, making her pulse flutter.

'That work can be your ticket out of anything,' he said. 'Anything at all.' He smiled at her, a half smile that was steely and determined. 'I just grabbed the coffee kiosk success and ran with it. Built it up, sold it, invested and started over. You can be in control of your own destiny through work. And that's why work will always come first with me.'

So that was why his relationships never amounted to anything. She saw now why their agreement had been of such use to him. She'd furthered his work. She'd provided a date so he didn't need to be distracted.

There had never been any prospect of him wanting more, then. She swallowed as she took that in.

'You'll meet someone one day who'll make you want to put work second,' she said. 'You won't know what you're missing until then.'

He shook his head.

'The moment someone becomes that important you start to lose focus. And things start to go wrong. I just don't need that kind of complication.'

She had the oddest feeling he wasn't just talking about overcoming his childhood.

'I think I'm going to turn in,' she said as they neared to the hotel. 'It's getting late now.'

The music continued on the terrace, more mellow now, and the crowd had dispersed a little. Adam stood to one side, mobile phone clamped to his ear, a stressed expression on his face.

That didn't come as any surprise to Dan. He could think of few things less stressful than getting married. Emma's parents were nowhere to be seen, but obviously just their presence on the premises was enough. In the centre of the terrace the ice sculpture continued its slow melt.

'I'll come with you,' he said.

The memory of kissing her danced slowly through his mind as they made their way inside. He'd known it might put her on edge—that had rather been the point...proof that he was calling the shots now. He hadn't thought it through any further than that. He hadn't counted on the way she would feel in his arms, all long limbs and fragile bone structure, such a contrast to the voluptuous curves that had always been his short-term fling diet. Or the way that satiny full lower lip would feel tugged between his own. There was a hotly curious part of him wondering how it might feel to take things further. He crushed that thought—hard.

His perception of her had changed. And not just because of the kiss but because of tonight. When had they ever discussed anything before that didn't have the ultimate goal of helping them in their jobs? It had been all insider tips from her. Who might be tendering for this contract, what their bid might be, who in her work circles might be looking for troubleshooting services. From him it had been handy introductions—name-dropping Emma to contacts who might want or need legal advice. All of it professional on one level or another.

This weekend was meant to be all about him taking charge, making the point that *he* was the one doing *her* the favour and then breaking off their arrangement the moment the wedding was over. The plan had seemed so easy in the wake of her insulting dumping of him—the perfect way to redress control and get rid of the gnawing feeling that he'd let her become indispensable in his life.

But the connection between them now felt more complex instead of more detached. The idea of walking away from it felt suddenly less gratifying. He'd been so busy taking what he could get from their agreement, manipulating it to suit his own ends so he could avoid close relationships, that he hadn't considered what might be in it for *her* beyond the shallow work reasons they both had.

For Emma it had been a way of making life easier.

Because to be 'good enough' she believed she had to fit a certain stereotype. He wasn't sure which was worse— using their agreement to escape past failures or using it to avoid any remote likelihood of ever having any.

As they walked up the stairs to their room Emma realised suddenly that he still had his arm loosely draped around her. There was no one around them to see it. No family members, no staff. Just what did that mean? Or did it mean anything at all?

She wondered if it felt as natural to him as it felt to her and gave herself a mental slap for even *thinking* about reading something into it. Really? This was Dan—Mr Two-Week Relationship himself. Even if that arm resting on her shoulders right now meant something—which it didn't—it would only ever be that.

Nothing meant anything to Dan Morgan except his work. He'd made that crystal clear this evening. And she wasn't in the market for anything that could be described as a fling. What would be the point? She'd had that with Alistair. What she wanted was not to be some throwaway bit of arm candy but to feel special, to come first, and she wasn't going to get that from Dan.

A hot kiss followed by a night sharing a room with him… The stuff of her dreams a few months ago. And now she had it, it was all for show. How par for the course of her life. They'd been alone together *loads* of times and he'd never had any intention of making a move. Pretend Emma got the hot kiss and the envious glances from female wedding guests over her gorgeous male companion. Real Emma got the awkwardness of bunking in with a work colleague.

She wriggled away from his arm and fumbled in her bag for the room key.

It had taken *months* to get over her stupid crush on him and to reinstate it now would be madness. She was just flustered, that was all, over a stupid fake kiss and a bit of a personal conversation. It didn't mean *anything*.

CHAPTER SEVEN

WHEN HAD HE last shared a bedroom with someone for a reason that had nothing to do with sex? Dan couldn't actually remember. It must have been Maggie. Way back when he was still at college and anything had seemed possible.

Had he now become so accustomed to room-sharing being about sex that his body simply expected it as part of the deal? Was that why he felt so damned on edge as he waited for Emma to change in the bathroom? Every nerve in his body was wound into a tense knot.

The air of awkwardness from earlier was back. But now there seemed a new, deeper edge to it. It was more than just the logistics of sharing a small space with someone you only knew on a work basis. His growing attraction to her was heightened by his new understanding of her. A few feet away from him in the velvet-soft darkness she would be there, lying in that bed, with her long, slender limbs and her silky dark hair.

His body matched his racing mind with a rigid, hot tension the like of which was going to make sleep an impossibility.

His pulse jolted as the bathroom door clattered open and she crossed the room to the bed, not looking at him.

Her dress was now lying over one arm, her hair loose and gleaming in the soft glow of the table lamp next to the bed. She was wearing a sleep vest and shorts which showed off the most impossibly perfect pair of long, slender legs.

He made an enormous effort not to stare at them as his mind insisted on wondering what other glorious secrets she might be hiding under her sensible work dresses and wide-leg trousers. He stared hard out of the window. His preoccupation became slightly less fake as he noticed movement in the grounds.

'Is that your brother down there?'

He immediately regretted mentioning it because she tossed the dress over the back of a chair and crossed the room to join him at the window, padding across the deep carpet in bare feet. What he *really* needed right now, with his entire body wound up like a coiled spring, was her standing next to him in her flimsy shorts and vest combo. Without her heels she just about reached his shoulder…

'Where?'

He pointed and she craned closer to him to see the lily pond bench. A figure was sitting and staring at the ground contemplatively, a bottle of champagne in one hand and a glass in the other. Her sudden nearness let Dan pick up the faint trace of vanilla perfume still clinging to her hair and his stomach gave a slow and delicious flip in response.

'It's Adam, all right,' she said. 'Even in silhouette that quiff is unmistakable. He's probably taking a break from negotiating family. Can't say I blame him.'

The soft breeze drifting in through the open window

ruffled her hair lightly. She turned away from the view and smiled up at Dan.

'Don't snore,' she said, her eyes teasing.

'I *don't* snore.'

She was close enough that in one swift tug she could be in his arms. He swallowed hard, his throat paper-dry.

Oblivious, she narrowed her eyes at him, considering.

'How do you know?'

'I've never had any complaints,' he said. Her lips, scrubbed of lip gloss, were a soft pale pink in the muted light. His eyes were drawn to them.

'That doesn't mean you don't snore,' she said. 'It just means no one's wanted to put you off them by telling you.'

'Whereas you…?'

'Will have no compunction whatsoever about lobbing a pillow at you.' She pressed an emphatic finger against his chest that made a wave of heat pulse through his veins. 'I'm not afraid to tell you what I think.'

'I know.'

For some reason the novelty of that was alluring. It occurred to him that the willingness to please of his usual girlfriends was something else besides easy and no-fuss. It was also very bland. When had he last felt on his toes with a woman?

He'd become slowly more aware of her looks this evening: the fragility of her skinny frame, her dark-hair-pale-skin combo—such a contrast to his usual choice—and now there was her liveliness, her cheek, sucking him in all the more.

For the first time he picked up on her physical similarities to Maggie. She was taller and slimmer, but the smooth dark hair was the same. Was that what this was about? Was that why she seemed to have slipped through his careful filter? Was that why it had been so easy to keep her at a distance and categorise her as a work colleague? Because his knee-jerk avoidance of any thought of attraction to a girl who might remind him of Maggie had gone on so long it had become automatic?

But he hadn't had the complication of being at such close quarters with her back then. Nuances and habits were laid bare now. The fun-loving, cheeky side of her was so much more obvious outside the work environment, where everything needed to be serious and professional. This weekend he'd begun to see what lay beneath. And it drew him in as no woman had. Not since Maggie had walked away.

She was smiling cheekily up at him, her brown eyes wide, and he marvelled again at how softly pretty she was when you took the time to look past her stiff outer layer. Her face was tilted up to his, at the perfect angle for him to kiss her. The warm, sweet scent of her hair filled his senses, and without taking time to think he lifted a hand to touch her cheek—just to see if it felt as satiny as it looked.

That one tiny connection with her gave his pulse an immediate leap and hot desire rushed through him. And in that fleeting moment he knew he had no chance.

Knowing he was acting off-plan now—and not just off-plan for this weekend but for his whole damned philosophy on life—was suddenly not enough to stop him. His mental filters weren't working. She'd already got past them. This was physical now, and there was nothing he could do about it.

Her eyes widened as he let his fingers trace further, around to the soft skin at the nape of her neck, beneath the fall of her hair. All thought of consequences gone, he lowered his mouth towards the silk of that tantalisingly full lower lip. He pulled her closer, melded her body hard against his, felt the contours of her long, slender limbs through the thin cotton of the shorts and vest she wore.

Sparks of hot longing fizzed in his abdomen as he let his hand slide lower, to find the soft cream of those long, slender thighs. Desire flooded through him, deeper than he was used to, steeped in the familiarity of her, the laughs they'd had together, their newfound closeness. This was not his usual throwaway date. He'd stepped outside the norm. The very novelty of that seemed to hike up his want for her to a new level.

A squeak of shock caught in Emma's throat as his thumb stroked along her jawline, his fingers tangling in her hair.

She hadn't imagined the shift in balance between them after all. She hadn't been seeing things that weren't there.

Despite all the flirting and the signs, the new feeling of intimacy as they started to get to know each other beyond the barriers of their previous life, she now realised that she'd never truly believed he could ever be interested in her. Not in *that* way. She'd quit any delusions about that months ago as she'd observed his repetitive dating habits, certain that unless she happened to morph overnight into a pouting curvy blonde, boring old plain Emma Burney simply wouldn't do it for him.

Her pulse had upped its pace so acutely that she felt light-headed. As his lips met hers she could taste a faint twist of champagne on them, warming her mouth as his tongue slipped softly against hers. Hot sparks began to tingle their way through her limbs to simmer hotly between her legs.

How many times had she dreamed of this moment in the dim and distant past when they'd first met? Every nerve-ending was tinglingly aware of him. She was drowning, every sense in her body filled with him. The lingering spicy notes of his aftershave made her senses reel. She let her fingers sink into his hair, its thick, soft texture exactly as she'd imagined it so many times.

The desire that had bubbled beneath the surface of her consciousness until she had abandoned all hope of it ever being reciprocated made a heady comeback, and she grabbed at the last thread of sense before it slipped away.

It was utterly, sublimely delicious, but none of it really counted because he was ending their agreement.

She latched on to that thought. Was that what all this had been about? The warmth of his newfound support and interest in her had delighted her, but she'd assumed it was simply down to friendship. His kiss was something she'd dreamed of, but if he'd wanted to snog her because of *her* he'd had *months* to do it.

All those months waiting for him to notice her, taking extra care with her hair and make-up when she knew she was going to see him, dropping everything to fit in his last-minute work dates. Months when he'd barely noticed she was alive. Months of opportunity, time alone together, work dinners out. None of it had been enough because he'd needed her for work then.

It had taken *this* for him to make a move on her. The fact that he was ending their agreement and had no need for her any more. Dan only slept with dispensable women. And now she was dispensable.

None of this had anything to do with real feelings for her.

With a monumental effort she stopped her arms from entwining around his neck and groped for his hands, grabbing them at the wrists and disentangling herself from his embrace. The sensation of loss as she took a step back made her suck in a sharp breath and she steeled herself against it. She was *not* going to be sucked into another bad decision because of some stupid age-old crush. She was in full control here.

'Why now?' she panted at him.

His eyes seemed a darker blue than ever, a light frown of confusion touching his forehead. She could hear that his breath had deepened.

He reached for her.

'What do you mean, why now?'

She took another step back, away from his hands, because if she found herself in those arms again she wasn't sure her resolve would stand up.

'We've known each other for months,' she said. 'And in all that time you've never looked twice my way. No matter what I did. No matter how many times I swung business deals for you or put myself out on your behalf. No matter how I tried. And then you decide we're going to go our separate ways, and out of the blue suddenly I'm fair game? Well, I'm not interested.'

She took a slow step back, shaking her head, avoiding his eyes, looking everywhere except at his face. Everything about her told him a very different story. Her shortness of breath, the flushed cheeks, the hard points of her nipples beneath the thin fabric of her vest.

His mind zeroed in on her words. *'No matter what I did.'* The meaning of that slammed into his brain and turned it to mush. Their agreement had always been about more than platonic convenience for her and he'd never even noticed. His stupid work tunnel vision had neglected to pick up on that point. The surge of excitement it now evoked shocked him to the core, telling him his belief that he was in control here was seriously misplaced.

'I'm not going to be your alternative choice because there's no handy blonde available and you're stuck sharing a room with me,' she said.

Clearly, to her, he was the same old work-obsessed confirmed bachelor.

'This has nothing to do with that.'

She gazed up at him, wariness in her wide brown eyes, and then they both jumped at a sudden flurry of knocks on the bedroom door.

She took a couple of fast paces away from him, her fingers rubbing slowly over her lips as if echoing his kiss. Another surge of desire flooded through him at the sight. She cut her eyes away from his.

Another mad cacophony of knocks sliced through the tension.

She made an exasperated noise and turned away from him towards the door, one hand pushing her hair back from her face in a gesture of fluster.

'Who the hell is that?'

'Emma, ignore it,' he said. 'We need to sort this out. You've got it wrong.'

The knocking graduated to a muffled banging of the kind a fist might make, and she shook her head lightly at him and moved towards the door again.

He glanced down at himself. In a sudden flash of clarity it occurred to him that the visitor might feasibly be Emma's mother, and his arousal would be obvious to her in the space of one look. He glanced at the door to the *en-suite* bathroom, thinking vaguely that he might take refuge in there for a couple of minutes while Emma got rid of whoever it was and then they could pick up where they'd left off.

He was on his way across the room when she opened the door and Adam, who had clearly been leaning on it, stumbled into the room, performed a twisty lurching pirouette and threw up into the nearest pot plant.

Oh, just bloody *perfect!*

'For Pete's sake, help me get him to the bathroom!'

Emma had managed to pull Adam to his extremely unsteady feet and struggled to hold him upright as he lurched about. Dan rushed in and took over, throwing one of her brother's arms around his neck and heaving him into the bathroom before he could collapse again. She followed them in.

'The wedding's off!' Adam groaned, slumping over the sink. His always-perfect hair hung in a dishevelled mess and his face was a sickly shade of green.

'What the hell's happened?' she said.

He lifted his head and pointed an emphatic jabbing finger at her as he swayed drunkenly.

'I'm a has-been, darling,' he drawled. 'It's all over. It's all gone.'

His knees gave way unexpectedly and Dan made a lunge to catch him before he hit the white-tiled floor.

'He's absolutely wasted,' Emma said, staring down at him. 'What the hell do I do?'

'Call down to Room Service,' Dan said. 'Black coffee. He needs to sober up.'

She left the pair of them in the bathroom and went to use the phone, her mind reeling. She'd never seen Adam lose his cool before. He had no worries that she knew of. His life was only ever full of things to celebrate. As she replaced the receiver there was the sound of gushing water from the bathroom and a piercing shriek of shock. Dan had obviously stuck him in the shower. She grinned in spite of her worry. Whatever she had to cope with now, at least Adam might be more lucid.

Adam emerged from the bathroom, still hideously pale, but his shocked eyes were now wide and staring. Water dripped from his face and his hair and he was clutching a towel and madly rubbing it at his front.

Dan followed him, his hands spread apologetically. 'Look, I'm sorry,' he said. 'I know cold water's a bit of a shock to the system, but it's great for sobering you up and I couldn't think what else to do.'

'Cold?' Adam wailed. 'It's not the bloody *cold*!' He cast horrified hands downwards at his sopping wet purple suit. 'What the hell have you done? This jacket's *designer!*'

CHAPTER EIGHT

Dan turned over for the fiftieth time on the sofa, knees bunched up because the damn thing was too short for him. Unfortunately that wasn't the only reason why sleep was totally elusive. The way Emma had felt in his arms had been far too delicious, far too enticing, for him to simply brush it out of his mind. Add in to that the way she'd put an end to it without having time to give a proper explanation and every nerve in his body was on full-scale alert, his arousal refusing to stand down even in her absence.

And, as interruptions went, needy family crises just about ticked his worst possible box. His stomach lurched between desire for her and the more rational desire to run a mile. It was bad enough to be in the middle of a huge family event when the last thing you wanted to be reminded of was the fact that you couldn't actually *do* family. He'd thought he was holding his own on that front pretty well, but now family complications were seeping in at every turn and he couldn't think of anything worse...

Somewhere in the small hours, after he'd finally given up on her returning to the room—not that it had made any change to his sleepless state—there was a soft click as the door opened. The benefit of his eyes being used to the velvet darkness meant he could watch the silhouette of her every move, while she had to feel her stumbling way from one piece of furniture to the next. Had he ever been more wide awake?

She muffled a yelp as she tripped over a chair and he took pity on her and reached to turn on the table lamp. She blinked at him in the muted golden light. She wore a sweater over her sleep shorts and vest that wasn't long enough to hide her gorgeous legs. His pulse immediately picked up where it had left off a couple of hours ago.

He heard her sigh as she clocked that he was still awake. He watched her run a hand through her already dishevelled hair as she sat down hard on the bed. Her face was a pale oval and there were dark shadows of tiredness beneath her eyes.

'You're still up,' she said.

He sat up on the sofa, the sheet bunched around his waist.

'I wasn't sure you were coming back tonight,' he said.

'Neither was I,' she said. 'I think Adam's drained the hotel's supply of black coffee.'

'He's sobered up, then?'

She nodded.

'He's sobered up. I thought that stuff about calling off the wedding was just cold feet—the usual night-before thing, down to him having drunk too much champagne. But there's more to it than that.'

She held his gaze for a moment.

'He's in financial trouble, Dan,' she said.

Worry etched her face and tugged at his heart.

'He's going under unless he can come up with a plan pretty damn quick.'

'For Pete's sake, what's he gone and done now? Spent a huge wad on a purple Bentley?'

She didn't smile.

He sat up straighter.

'Didn't you tell me his pictures sell for five figures?' he said, scratching his head and trying to think clearly. Tiredness was kicking in now. He had absolutely no desire to discuss Adam's spending habits at two in the morning.

'One of his pictures was supposed to. A month or so ago. Adam borrowed a wodge of cash on the back of it and then the sale fell through. He's been so in vogue recently that even *he* believed the hype. Instead of being productive he's been spending money he doesn't have like water. A new swanky flat here, a shedload of designer furniture there… And now things have reached breaking point. He only found out this afternoon.'

'Can't Ernie bail him out? I thought his family were swimming in cash.'

She frowned at him.

'That's exactly why he doesn't want to *tell* Ernie. He doesn't want him to think he's marrying him for a bail-out. And, more than that, he doesn't want Ernie to think he's a failure. You can't imagine what that means to Adam—he never fails at anything. *Ever.* He's refusing to change his mind about calling off the wedding. It was all I could do to make him promise not to do anything until the morning. I need to think of a way to persuade him by then.'

Dan looked at the worry darkening her face and saw a flash of hope in her eyes as she fixed them on his.

'What he really needs is some sound business advice,' she said, with a pointed tone to her voice that really wasn't necessary. 'From someone who knows what they're doing.'

She wanted him to step in. The unspoken request hung in the air as clearly as if she'd shouted it.

Cold clarity immediately took over his brain with the automatic response that had been honed and conditioned in him over the course of the last ten years.

Not his problem.

He didn't *do* family problems. That was actually the one big advantage of not having a family—not getting sucked into other people's dramas, not having anyone rely on him for help. He'd thought he'd done a pretty good job of distancing himself from the blasts from the past that the whole family wedding ambience kept lobbing his way this weekend, but this was a step too far.

'You want *me* to talk to him?' He could hear the note of frosty defensiveness in his own voice. 'I'm not convinced that would be a good idea. It's his private business—nothing to do with me. He needs to discuss it with Ernie. Isn't that the whole point of marriage—shared problems and all that?'

He dropped his eyes from hers so he wouldn't see the disappointment seeping into them. He ran a hand awkwardly through his hair.

'There isn't going to *be* a marriage unless someone gets him back on track,' she hissed.

'What makes you think that someone should be *me*? I don't think Adam would thank you for involving a stranger in his personal problems. This isn't down to me,' he said.

'A stranger?'

He glanced up and caught her gaze again. Bitter disappointment lurked there. Deep in his stomach a spike of regret kicked in unexpectedly at the idea of letting her down. He steeled himself against it. He shouldn't care about this.

She paused a beat too long, during which he held his position and didn't give in, and then she exploded.

'Fine. Absolutely fine,' she snapped, leaping to her feet.

Had she really thought he would step up to the plate? Why the *hell* had she assumed that? Because he'd kissed her? After months of zero romantic interest he'd kissed her. OK, so she'd thought there had been something more than their usual work relationship growing between them this last day or so, but clearly she'd imagined that. Her first instincts had been spot on and she'd been totally right to stop him in his tracks.

Her mistake had been in hoping that what was between them was in any way about more than the kiss and what he'd obviously intended to follow that kiss up with if Adam hadn't interrupted them spectacularly.

'You didn't even ask me what was wrong with Adam,' she said dully. Her head ached tiredly and she rested her hand against her scalp, lacing her fingers through her hair to pull the roots back from her face, trying to clear her thoughts. 'I thought you were waiting up for me all this time to make sure I was OK, to be supportive, but you weren't actually wondering for one second what the problem was. If I hadn't just told you, you would never have asked me about Adam, would you?'

She glanced down at her fingers.

'That's not what you were waiting up for at all, is it? You just wanted to pick up where we left off earlier. You thought I'd sort Adam out, get him over his hissy fit, and then we'd have the rest of the night to make it into that bed.'

She nodded across the room at the four-poster.

For a moment she got no response and she raised her eyebrows at him expectantly. See if he could talk his way out of this. Or if he would even be bothered to try.

'This has nothing to do with what happened earlier,' he said, not meeting her eyes. 'I just think Adam is big enough to sort out his own problems. I don't get why you need to get sucked into this. His overspending isn't down to you.'

She stared at him, incredulous at his lack of concern.

'Because that's what families do,' she said. 'You know, I always thought nothing could ever touch Adam. He's led a charmed life. As if everything he ever touches is sprinkled with happy dust. When I was a kid I sometimes used to wish for just one time when he would stuff up, show everyone that he wasn't perfect.'

She paused briefly, thinking of how upset Adam was now. There was no joy in that for her. She wasn't a stupid kid any more.

'For once I'm not the one who's screwed up, but I have no good feeling about that. What good would it do if my parents knew what had happened? I just want him to go back to his usual crazy self.'

She made a conscious effort to curb her voice. It was so late now the hotel was pin-drop quiet. Every word she spoke felt amplified in the silence.

'Of course you do,' he said. 'You're comfortable in his shadow, so you're hardly about to want that shadow to get smaller, are you?'

She stared at him.

'Just what the hell is *that* supposed to mean?' She

wanted to shout it. Her voice felt shaky on her tongue. She kept her tone measured with great difficulty.

He shrugged.

'It's safer, isn't it? Believing that you're always going to be inferior? Means you don't have to put yourself out there. You rely on Adam being the star that he is in every possible way because it's an excuse for you to take the safe option.'

'That's not true.'

'Isn't it? Look at our plus-one agreement. I know what *I* was getting out of it—easy networking, work contacts. But what about you? Your dates were all about presenting a front to your family, because that way you didn't have to put yourself there in reality. With me you couldn't fail.'

For a moment she had trouble comprehending what he meant because it came as such a shock. A sharp, hot lurch hit her in the stomach. She shoved away the thought that this was what it felt like to have someone touch a nerve. Refusing to engage in one-upmanship with Adam was a way of avoiding grief from her over-interested parents, *not* a way to embrace the safe option because she was afraid of failure.

Dan saw the dark, defensive anger flush her face and wondered for a moment if he'd gone too far. She'd made him feel such a lightweight for not pitching in instantly to help Adam—who, frankly, was responsible for his own cock-up. Discomfort at the situation had stopped him holding back, and second thoughts seeped in a moment too late.

Her hands flew to her hips, her eyes flashed in anger

and her previous attempts to speak in a low voice went totally out of the window.

'You're twisting things!' she yelled. 'I don't know where the hell you get off, preaching to me about family bloody values. Your concern gene is mutated. All this has been about—all anything has *ever* been about for you—is getting someone into bed. In this case, in the absence of any willing curvy blondes, that happens to be me. Well, I'm not interested in being one of your dispensable little-black-book girlies. I don't need you as a boyfriend—not even as a fake one. If this wedding goes ahead—which, the way it looks right now, is unlikely—I'll go it alone. I don't need you. So first thing in the morning you can get back to your sad workaholic singleton life in London.'

He'd never seen her lose her temper. Her voice shook with the force of it and she stood at her full height, her eyes wide and her cheeks flushed. Even in his amazement at her overreaction—which told him he'd not only touched a nerve but had held on to it and twisted it hard—the most visceral part of him zeroed in on how utterly beautiful she looked in that animated moment.

Then admiration fell flat as she turned her back on him, stalked into the bathroom and slammed the door so hard he was surprised the hotel didn't collapse into rubble around them.

Not the delicious uninhibited night of passion he'd expected when he'd kissed her a few hours earlier. Admittedly at the time his mind hadn't been working ahead by more than a few minutes. He certainly hadn't thought about the consequences—it had been very easy to discount those. Any possible repercussions had seemed very far away when the silk of her skin had been beneath his fingers.

If he'd been lying in a regular bed he would have been ramrod-straight. Instead he was cramped into a hunch with his knees up. His body was one big throb of pent-up sexual energy. Every muscle was tightly coiled up with it. And did he really think he could pass the whole night like this?

She'd spent an hour in the bathroom before she'd re-emerged into the darkened room and stalked past him into bed. No attempt to make conversation. Now a silver shaft of moonlight filtered through a chink in the curtains and fell on her bare shoulder as she lay with her back to him. The long legs were drawn up; she was curled beneath the sheet.

For an endless length of time he had felt sure, despite her silence, that she was awake. Her angry vibe had been palpable. Tension still filled the room. He shifted again, in a vain attempt to get comfortable, and wondered what exactly he was bothering with all this for.

He should be looking on Adam's rubbish timing as a very fortuitous wake-up call, shouldn't he? He'd been completely focused on the overwhelming physical pull of her. If he'd stopped for a second to analyse it he would have assumed it would be a one-night stand. After all, he'd made it clear that their agreement had run its course, and that had removed any benefit of keeping things platonic between them. He'd been thinking quick weekend fling.

Hadn't he?

If his interest in her was purely physical, dispensable, then why did her furious criticism of him gnaw at his insides like this? He had no obligation to her or her family, and yet somehow she'd managed to instil guilt because he didn't want to get involved in Adam's undoubtedly crazy problems.

He didn't *do* guilt. That was one of the main benefits of keeping his relationships shallow. He and Emma didn't even *have* a relationship and he couldn't bloody sleep. He had no idea how she'd managed to do this to him.

There was a part of him that was halfway back to London in his head already, keen to do exactly as she had suggested.

She shifted gently in her sleep and he sat up on the sofa, throwing back the crumpled sheet. He could see the smooth pool of her dark hair on the pillow. The quality of the light in the room had changed almost imperceptibly and he glanced at the luminous face of his watch. Dawn would be kicking in before he knew it. He could be back in his Docklands flat in an easy couple of hours if he left now. No need to battle London traffic if he left this early. Why the hell was he even still here?

You want to help. You want this involvement with her and her family.

He absolutely *did not.*

Every sensible instinct told him to get some serious distance from this situation but he rationalised furiously. A brief chat with Adam—and a brief chat was all it *would* be, too—might be the perfect way to take control of this situation. He wasn't about to quietly slink back to London on her say-so, leaving her with the upper hand.

He ignored the inner voice whispering that he didn't like being labelled as selfish, because labels were to him completely irrelevant. Results mattered. Successes.

Not good or bad opinions. Even if they happened to be *her* opinions.

Help Adam out and Emma would be in his debt. The fact that after that kiss she felt very much like unfinished business was beside the point. He was not about to fall for her. He was in total control here. When they got back to London he would end their agreement, as planned, in full possession of the moral high ground. It wasn't as if she wasn't expecting him to. He'd made it clear this was their last outing together. There would be no need to see her again after that. It would be over.

There was a chink in the curtains that let the sunlight in.

It took a moment for her brain to process the fact that the bedroom window of her flat in Putney looked out onto a tiny enclosed yard which the sun penetrated for roughly ten minutes somewhere around noon. Additional details seeped into her consciousness. This bed was hard, where hers was soft, and was that *birdsong* she could hear? Where was the roar of rush-hour traffic?

This was *not* her flat in Putney.

Reality rushed in. Luxury country house hotel. Adam's mad-as-a-box-of-frogs wedding. Disastrous room-share with her crush of the year.

She sat bolt upright and stars swam in front of her eyes at the unexpected movement. She turned instantly to look at the sofa. Every bone in her body ached with tension and her eyes felt gritty when she blinked. She could have sworn she'd been awake all night. Yet that couldn't be so. Last seen lying on the sofa as she climbed back into bed at two-thirty and turned her back on him in fury, at some point Dan had managed to get up and exit the room without her noticing.

She checked the time and that was enough to get her out of bed in a split second. How the hell had she managed to sleep in? Her stomach kicked into churning with a sudden sense of urgency. She needed to get up, check on Adam and find out if the wedding was going ahead or not.

The thought of dealing with the fallout if his world imploded filled her with dread. Adam would be in the doghouse and the spotlight would be right back on her life—her failure to keep a man, her failure to produce grandchildren. Her mind stuttered on that thought with a sharp stab of shame. Surely her only concern should be for Adam, for how she could best help him sort out the mess that was his life, how she could support him through the stress. The thought of the effect it might have on *her* shouldn't even be entering her mind.

Dan's accusation from the previous night rose darkly in her mind. Could he have a point about her living in Adam's shadow because it was safer there?

She crossed the room swiftly to the *en-suite* bathroom, knowing from the silence that Dan wasn't there but sticking her head around the door anyway to check.

Nothing.

She glanced at the hotel information brochure on top of the bureau. Breakfast had been running for at least an hour already—maybe he'd gone down to the dining room. The possibility that he'd upped and left lurked at the very edge of her consciousness but she delayed any consideration of it. And then, as she turned, her eyes took in the antique desk and her heart gave a miserable lurch that she refused to acknowledge.

His holdall wasn't in the room. And, worse, nor were

his laptop and all the associated office stuff which basically provided his identity. All of it was gone.

She threw on jeans and a T-shirt and speed-walked down the deep-carpeted hall to the honeymoon suite. Ernie had spent the previous night at his parents' home and had planned to get ready there, so Adam should still be alone.

He opened the door on her first knock and stood aside to let her in before crossing the room back to the full-length mirror. He was wearing an ivory crushed velvet slim-cut suit with gold piping and super pointy shoes that even *she* would think twice about squashing her toes into. He looked her up and down, an eyebrow cocked.

'I do hope you're not wearing that,' he said, waving a hand at her jeans-and-old-T-shirt combo. 'This is a classy event.'

'Of course I'm not wearing this,' she snapped.

There was something incredibly exasperating about the way he was acting, as if the events of the previous night had never happened when they'd caused her a stress-fest of monumental proportions.

'I didn't see the point in putting on a swanky wedding outfit and doing my hair when the likelihood of it going ahead was somewhere around fifty-fifty. At least it was when I left you in the small hours.'

She sat down on the enormous bed. Everything in the honeymoon suite was supersized, albeit in a country hotel kind of a way. The four posts were taller, the swags of fabric bedecking them were bigger and sweepier, and through the door of the *en suite* she could see an enormous sunken bath.

'Oh, that!'

Adam flapped a dismissive hand at her and turned

back to his reflection in the mirror. He looked a little tired and drawn but otherwise remarkably like his usual upbeat self. She caught sight of her own reflection behind him. She looked an exhausted wreck. How bloody unfair.

'That's all sorted now.'

She stared at him in disbelief.

'What about last night's meltdown?' His lack of re-action combined with her tiredness made her temper strain to breaking point. 'You puked in my plant, for Pete's sake! You had a total emotional meltdown. Your life was *over*.'

'Oh, that,' he said again, glancing back at her.

At least he had the good grace to look sheepish now.

'Sorry about that, sweetie. Glass of champagne too many. Still, there were compensations. In fact some might say it had elements of stag night perfection.'

He grinned at her mystified expression.

'Sharing a shower room with the gorgeous Dan, for example,' he said mischievously, spraying a toothbrush with hairspray and smoothing his already perfect quiff into place. 'Even if he did ruin my suit.' He tapped the side of his nose with one finger in a your-secret's-safe-with-me gesture. 'Lucky old you. I know you thought you hit the jackpot with Alistair Woods, but I've always thought Dan was in a league of his own. Nice work.' He winked at her and turned back to the top of the bureau, which was groaning under the weight of male grooming products. 'I never did think Lycra cycle wear was a good look—didn't like to mention it.'

He lavishly sprayed a five-foot-high cloud of oriental spiced aftershave into the room beside him and stepped into it.

Emma pinched her nose to stifle a sneeze. She shook her head in automatic denial.

'It's not like that. We're just work friends.'

He cackled mad laughter.

'Sure you are! That's why he's just given me an *enormous* business loan with zero interest and his personal phone number so I can tap him for strategic advice whenever I need it.' He winked. 'Either that or maybe he's got the hots for *me*. Maybe you've got competition, sweetie.'

She stared at him in disbelief and he obviously mistook incredulity for angry possessiveness.

'I'm joking!' He held his hands up and laughed. 'For Pete's sake, where's your sense of humour?'

'When?' she said, as if in a dream. 'When did he do all this? His stuff's gone from the room. I can't find him anywhere.' She paused. 'We had a bit of a disagreement.'

Adam shook his head.

'He'll be back. He turned up here around dawn, woke me up, ordered a gallon of black coffee and forced me to come clean about my debts.' He coloured a little. 'It wasn't pretty. Then he talked me through a business plan for the next three years and touted unbelievable terms for a loan. I thought he'd want a cut of everything I make for life at the very least, and I would have agreed to it, too. Frankly, I would have put up my *granny* as security to dig me out of this hole. But no.' He shook his head wonderingly. 'He is *so* into you.' He pointed the toothbrush at her.

Her brain was spinning, trying to process what all this meant.

'Where is he now, then? He didn't come back to the room.'

Adam shrugged. 'Around, I think. He was going to make a few calls, draw up some papers and get the ball rolling. I'm sure he'll show up once it's all organised, sweetie. He's probably in the lobby soaking up the free Wi-Fi.'

Or en route back to the city and deliberately avoiding her. Her heart gave a half plummet at the thought and she gritted her teeth. She tugged her fingers through her hair, as if she could somehow smooth some sense into her muddled brain.

She'd told him to go back to London and instead he'd stayed to put together a bail-out package for Adam. Her heart turned over meltingly and she desperately tried to rein it in, to come up with an alternative explanation to the one that was slamming into her brain.

He'd done this for her.

He'd done it to prove her wrong about him.

She cringed inwardly as she remembered the awful things she'd said to him in the throes of her enormous meltdown tantrum. What possible other explanation could there be? It was way above and beyond Dan's normal remit. Dan didn't step in to fix other people's crises. Ever. Since he kept the world at arm's length it was usually impossible to get close enough to his shoulder to cry on it.

He'd stepped outside the box. And what the hell was she meant to make of that?

CHAPTER NINE

DAN RAN A hand through his hair distractedly as his phone kicked in for the third time in the last ten minutes. Each of the calls had been from Emma. For the third time he pressed 'call reject' on the dashboard and fixed his expression on the road. The motorway would still be pretty clear this time of the morning, but he'd hit traffic when he reached London. It was a Saturday so would be marginally better.

Dealing with Adam had taken a good deal longer than he'd thought it would. Still, it was done now. Loan organised, cash transfer organised, soul sold. Point made. The wedding would go ahead without a hitch and he would return to his work in London. The ridiculous plus-one agreement would be discharged exactly as he'd planned. They would move forward separately, but Emma would go with the knowledge that she'd been wrong about him.

Sad workaholic singleton.

Was that really what he boiled down to? His mind gnawed at it relentlessly and, try as he might, he couldn't shake the feeling that the reason it bothered him so much was because *she'd* said it. He, who didn't give a toss about how he came across to people so long as the job got done, *cared* what she thought of him.

A miserable, dark churning was kicking into his stomach with every mile he drove further away.

Emma pelted back up the stairs for the third time, having performed a whirlwind circuit of all the public rooms and lounges in the hotel, her heart sinking lower by the second. The marquee was teeming with hotel staff transforming it from plain tent into what was, by the look of it, to be some kind of yellow-themed fairy grotto, all under the supervision of a pristinely dressed wedding coordinator with a clipboard and a voice like a sergeant major.

There wasn't another guest in sight, she hadn't showered, washed her hair or applied a dab of make-up, and she only had an hour or so left to get ready before pre-wedding cocktails and nibbles were served. Her mother was probably already wearing her mother-of-the-bride outfit and preparing herself for an afternoon of wedding critique. Wherever Dan had disappeared to, catching up with him and sorting things out would have to go maddeningly on hold now that the wedding was going ahead as planned.

Maybe he'd come back while she was getting dressed…

She showered and changed with minutes to spare and there was still no sign of him.

Maybe he had no intention of coming back at all while she was there. She had told him he was selfish for not helping out a friend, that he cared about no one but himself. Without him here there was only one conclusion. This wasn't about any regard for *her*—it was about making a point, showing her she was wrong about him and then exiting her life with the moral high ground.

The finished marquee turned out to be a yellow flower explosion. Huge floral arrangements stood on plinths in every spare space. Yellow silk bunting decked the roof, and the chairs were wrapped in huge yellow bows, standing in twin rows separated by a wide aisle covered with a thick-pile yellow carpet. At the very front a perfectly dressed white table was decked in yellow flowers.

She was one of the last people to take her seat, earning a glare from her mother, who was perched in the front row rubbernecking at the other guests. Her furious face was topped by an enormous salmon-pink feather hat which clashed eye-wateringly with the mad overuse of yellow.

In a sudden burst of exasperated defiance Emma stood straight up again. She could just nip outside and try his phone again. And maybe while she was there check the car park. At least that would be conclusive.

She sidestepped out of her row and turned back down the aisle to the door. She had to get hold of him. She wasn't about to let this go now—wedding or no wedding. She was stopped in her tracks by a deafening funked-up version of the 'Bridal March' as Adam and Ernie blocked the door in front of her. They were both wearing dark glasses, probably in defence against the major overuse of yellow. Ernie's small niece walked at their feet, lobbing yellow rose petals. The eyes of everyone in the room bored into her back and she had no choice but to slink back to her seat.

What was she thinking? She might as well face facts.

The wedding was under way. And he was clearly not coming.

The wave of sadness that realisation evoked took her breath away and made her throat constrict. The assumption that he'd helped Adam for her, because he *cared* about her, seemed unlikely now that he hadn't hung around to soak up her gratitude. The surge of excitement she'd felt when Adam had told her what had happened took a nosedive into stomach-churning disappointment. She would have to resign herself to coping with the ceremony and its aftermath by herself.

It was an odd novelty to be stressed about something else for a change, instead of the usual prospect of mad parental behaviour. The thought of being without him beat all her other problems into submission. Nothing seemed to bother her now. Her parents could do their worst, and probably would.

And then, just as she mentally gave up on Dan and tried to steel herself to get through the day without losing her sanity, her stomach gave an unexpected and disorientating flip as he walked into the marquee.

He strode casually down the aisle behind Adam and Ernie, crushing the trail of yellow rose petals under his feet, and slid into the seat next to her as if he was just a couple of minutes late instead of having gone AWOL for the last twelve hours. Any possible annoyance with him was immediately sidelined by her heart, which went into full thundering mode. To hide it, she immediately faked irritation.

She spoke from the corner of her mouth as Adam launched into his personally written over-emotional vows. Ernie was gazing at him adoringly.

'You're late,' she whispered.

He stared straight ahead. In his dark suit and crisp white shirt he looked ready for cocktails at some trendy London wine bar. A yellow carnation had been pinned to his lapel by one of the super-efficient attendants. There was a hint of stubble lining his jaw and one tiny sign that he'd cut it fine—the spikes of his hair were still slightly damp from the shower.

'I'm not. I'm bang on time.'

'I thought you'd gone back to London.'

This time he looked her way and gave her a half smile that made her stomach go soft.

'Just because you told me to? You don't get rid of me that easily.'

Her stomach gave a slow and delicious flip. What the hell did *that* mean? That he wanted to stay or that he was making a point?

The service progressed at the front of the room and she barely heard a word of it. Her mind continued to whirl while cheers rang out around them and a shower of yellow confetti fluttered over Adam and Ernie as they raised triumphant hands above their heads. She hardly took in any of it. All she wanted was to drag Dan somewhere quiet to talk.

Nerves twisted inside her as she followed the rest of the guests back up the yellow-ribbon-lined aisle and into the hotel's conservatory for drinks while the marquee was reset for dinner. A string quartet kicked into action at one side of the room as waiting staff with trays of canapés began to mingle with the guests. Dan nodded around, smiling and winking at people, working the fake plus-one wedding guest image to a tee, and suddenly she could stand it no longer.

She grabbed him by the elbow and tugged him to a quiet corner of the room.

'Where *were* you all morning, then?' she said. 'You don't get off that easily.'

She waited for him to regale her with how he'd single-handedly solved Adam's problems and then sit back to watch her eat her words.

Instead he shrugged easily and took a sip of his champagne.

'Around. I'm an early riser. You were dead to the world, snoring away.'

He grinned broadly as she aimed an exasperated slap at his shoulder.

'I do *not* snore.'

So he was clearly not immediately going to volunteer what he'd done. What was the point of actually *doing* it, then, if it hadn't been to impress her?

She ran her hand through her hair, trying to think straight. She was so confused.

Dan watched her over the rim of his glass, trying to maintain a relaxed air of mingling wedding guest when all he wanted to do was stare at her. She looked prettier than ever in a silver-grey silk dress that set off her creamy complexion. Her hair was lying in soft waves, one side held back from her face by a sparkly clip. His desire for her was as strong as it had been the previous night. Nothing had changed. Had he really thought it would?

She held his gaze boldly and he heard her take a deep breath.

'You helped Adam,' she said. 'I know about the loan. I thought you didn't want to get sucked into family stuff.'

He deliberately didn't meet her eyes and kept his tone light.

'Yeah, well, I wasn't thinking straight when you first suggested it,' he said. 'Maybe I just wasn't crazy on Adam's timing.'

He watched the blush rise on her cheeks at his reference to the previous night and heat began to pool deep in his abdomen.

'Well, if you think I'll just hop into bed with you now, because you stepped up to the plate with Adam, you're wrong,' she said.

If only that were the limit of his need for her.

'If I'd wanted to go to bed with someone I wouldn't have wasted half the night counselling Adam. I would have been down in the lobby chatting up the receptionist.'

If he needed any reminder that he was in over his head here, there it was. This was *not* just about getting her into bed.

He'd actually done far more than he'd intended when he'd left her sleeping in the small hours. The plan to just give Adam some kind of rousing pep talk had gone out of the window when he'd realised the monumental size of the mess he was in. Within five minutes it had become clear that a couple of websites and the number of a debt helpline were simply not going to cut the mustard, and the temptation had never been stronger to simply bow out of the situation and leave all of them to it while he went right back to his safe and organised life in London.

But all he'd been able to think about was Emma floundering the next morning, trying to pick up the pieces, and he simply hadn't been able to do it to her.

And what that decision meant filled him with far

more trepidation than practically writing out a blank check to her lunatic brother.

He had feelings for her. Beyond anything he'd felt since Maggie. And even she now seemed to be taking on a vagueness in his mind that she hadn't had before—as if the edges of her memory were being softened by the reality of the present.

'To prove a point, then,' she said, narrowing her eyes. 'You can't stand being wrong and I touched a nerve.'

He cocked an eyebrow.

'With your "sad workaholic singleton" comment, you mean? I think I've had a few worse insults than that over the years.'

'Then what? Why would you do that about-face if it wasn't so you could have the last word?'

The cynical tilt of her chin finally tipped him into irritation.

'I notice you haven't asked me if I just did it out of the goodness of my heart. It hasn't occurred to you that I might just want to *help*.'

'Of course it hasn't. Because there's always an ulterior motive with you. Normally it's to do with work. Or possibly sex.'

'Emma, are you so used to being second best that you have to find some negative reason when the truth is staring you in the face? Why is it that you can't possibly contemplate that I might have just done the whole bloody thing for *you?*' he blurted in exasperation. 'You're maddening, your family are insane, you snore and your luggage habits are scary. But for some reason I'd rather commit myself financially to your mad brother and stay here with you instead of going back to London and my nice, peaceful, "sad workaholic singleton" life. Do you think I don't want to run for the hills? Truth is, I can't. I've realised there's nowhere I'd rather be than here.' He paused for breath. 'With you.'

She was staring at him.

His pulse vaulted into action as he met her wide brown eyes. He could see the light flush on her cheekbones. All the unrequited tension of the night before seeped back through his body. All around them the socialising carried on, and the urge raced through him to ignore the lot of them, grab her by the hand and tug her upstairs—let this crazy charade go on without them.

He closed the gap between them and lifted a hand to her cheek. The softness of her skin was tantalising beneath his fingers.

'Dinner is served.'

The Master of Ceremonies' curt tones cut through the background buzz of chatter and snapped him out of it.

'Do stop dawdling, darling,' Emma's mother called as she swept past them in her ghastly coral ensemble, undoubtedly en route to the top table.

Oh, for Pete's sake…

By the time the meal was over the presence of Adam's entire social circle was beginning to seriously annoy Emma. It was extremely difficult to have an in-depth personal conversation while seated at a table of eight overenthusiastic art groupies.

Dinner finished with, the marquee was cleared of the tables in the centre to reveal a glossy dance floor. Strings of fairy lights and candelabra supplied a twinkly, magical ambience. You couldn't move without tripping over a champagne waiter. And this after the most sumptuous four-course meal she'd ever been too strung-out to eat. Clearly there had been no expense spared. She wondered just how big Dan's loan to Adam was. If this was the level of his spending habits he'd still be paying it off when he was drawing his pension.

'I mean, really—no speeches? No best man. No bridesmaids. No tradition whatsoever! I just want to *know*—and I'm sure I'm not alone in this—' her mother glanced around for confirmation '—what happens about the name-change? Who takes whose name?'

She looked expectantly at Adam, standing nearby, who shifted from foot to foot.

'Mum, it's no different to any other wedding. You can take or not take whatever name you please,' Emma said, pasting on a smile to counteract any offence that might be caused. 'You're living in the past.'

'I don't agree. I don't see why Adam should change his name.'

'I'm not,' Adam said. 'And neither is Ernie.'

Her mother rounded on Ernie, who took an automatic defensive step backwards.

'Why not?' she demanded. 'Is our family name not good enough?'

'Mum, please…' Emma said.

Ernie held his hands up.

'It's perfectly fine, Emma. It's nothing to do with family names.' He looked kindly at her mother. 'I'd walk over hot coals for him, darling, but I cannot possibly be known as Ernie Burney.'

Adam took his arm and they moved away. Her mother gaped for a moment, and then took refuge in her usual critical safe bet in order to save face.

'Of course if *you* could only find a man who would commit there wouldn't be any of this lunacy,' she snapped at Emma. 'We could have a proper wedding with all the trimmings.'

The band chose that moment to launch into full-on swing music, mercifully making it impossible to hear any further argument, and the compère took to the glossy parquet floor.

'Ladies and gentlemen, I give you…the groom and groom.'

Her mother's mouth puckered and then disappeared as a pool of light flicked on in the centre to reveal Adam and Ernie striking a pose. A kitsch disco track kicked into action and they threw themselves into a clearly pre-rehearsed dance routine.

Dan stared in amazement as Adam danced past them, finger stabbing the air above his head, back to his full quota of sweeping flamboyant enthusiasm. Ernie skidded across the parquet on his knees, snapping his fingers above his head. A circle of guests began to form at the edges of the dance floor, clapping along. The room worked itself into a crescendo of rhythmic toe-tapping. It was bedlam.

'And…the parents of the happy couple…'

Ernie's father, completely unaware of what he was letting himself in for, held out a hand to Emma's mother and began propelling her around the floor. Emma watched her mother's stiff and obvious fluster with a grin.

'She can't complain. She did want a bit more tradition after all,' she said.

'And…family and friends…please take the floor…'

Dan held his hand out, a smile crinkling his eyes. She stared at him, her heart skipping into action.

'I don't dance,' she said, shaking her head.

He totally ignored her. Before she could wriggle free

he'd caught her fingers in his own and tugged her against him, curling his free hand around her waist.

'Just hang on, then,' he said.

The jaunty music demanded a lot more balance and rhythm than a swaying slow dance, and Emma silently cursed Adam for his disco obsession.

Dan turned out to be an excellent dancer. He propelled her smoothly around the floor in perfect time to the music and she somehow managed to hold on to him instead of falling over. Then at last the music mercifully slowed and embarrassment slowly gave way to consciousness of him. She could feel the hard muscle of his thighs moving against her own. Sparks jumped from her fingers as he laced them through his. His heartbeat pressed against hers.

'Why now, then?' she said, looking up at him, a light frown shadowing her face. 'You haven't answered that question. You had *months* to make a move on me if you were interested. Months of work dates back in London. Why now? Why here? Because you'd made it clear our agreement was over? Is that it? You were pretty keen to draw a line under our relationship when this weekend finished, so did that make me fair game?'

'If I'd known you were interested maybe I would have made a move before,' he said, knowing perfectly well he'd never have allowed himself to do so.

She made an exasperated sound.

'That's crap. I'm *so* not your type.'

'In actual fact you're *exactly* my type. And that's why I never made a move. I met you in your work role and you were so bloody good at it I wasn't about to ruin that by sleeping with you. I needed you too much.'

She pulled away from him a little as she processed what that might mean.

'And now you don't need me any more, sleeping with me is suddenly back on the agenda? Is that it?'

'That's not it at all. This weekend is the first I've spent with anyone at such close quarters without sex being the only thing on the agenda. And it isn't a piece of cake, I'll be honest with you. Nothing about you is easy. You're a pain to share a room with, and your family are more bonkers than I realised, but for the first time in I don't know how long work isn't the first thing I'm thinking about.'

She looked up at him and met his eyes, his expression clear and genuine.

'When I talked to Adam I realised there would be a massive fallout if the wedding didn't go ahead. I could imagine the embarrassment, the fuss, having to send the guests away. It wasn't about Adam. He's got himself into trouble and he should dig himself out of it. It might even be character-building. When I couldn't walk away I realised that the person I was really doing it for was you. And that's when I knew that, whatever I felt about you, platonic work colleague didn't really cover it any more.'

He carried on talking, thinking vaguely that they seemed to have lost time with the jaunty beat of the music. Other guests began to whirl past them.

She stopped dancing. He attempted a couple more steps before giving up and joining her. The thing about dancing was that you needed your partner at least to *attempt* to engage—otherwise it was akin to dragging a sack of potatoes around the floor at speed. Trepidation spiked in his stomach at the look of disbelief on her face, telling him that his feelings for her had climbed way further than he'd thought. He'd been kind of banking on a smile at the very least.

'Say that again.'

'Emma, we're in the middle of the bloody dance floor. Let's go and sit down, get a drink.'

'I don't want a drink. Say that again.'

'I couldn't give a toss about Adam getting into trouble?'

She punched his shoulder.

'Not that bit.'

He saw the mock-exasperated smile on her lips, saw it climb to her eyes.

'Platonic work colleague didn't cover it any more?'

The smile melted away. She was looking up at him, brown eyes wide, soft lips lightly parted, and the madly circling dance floor around them disappeared from his consciousness.

'Yes. That bit.'

He tightened his grip around her waist and slid his fingers into her hair, stroking his thumb along her jawline as he tilted her lips to meet his.

Emma's heart was thundering as if they'd done another disco turn instead of swaying languorously around the dance floor.

The Dan she'd known for a year and long given up on would never have helped Adam out for nothing in return—would never have taken the time to explain his feelings to her. And he would never have turned back having driven halfway to London—not when he'd made his point before he left. She'd bucked his little-black-book no-strings trend. He'd put her first.

Sweet excitement began to swirl in her stomach as

her mind focused on the feel of his body hard against hers and she breathed in the scent of spicy aftershave and warm skin as he kissed and kissed and kissed her.

At last she opened her eyes to see the *déjà-vu* disapproving stare of her mother across the room. Necking on the dance floor, this time, instead of in corridors—how common. Except that this time she found she really couldn't give a *damn*.

She laced her hand through his and tugged at his arm. 'Let's go upstairs.'

CHAPTER TEN

SHE FOLLOWED HIM into the hotel room, buying a bit more time and space for her skittering nerves by leaning gently back against the door until it clicked shut. The party carried on in the marquee below them and music and faint laughter drifted in through the window, open a crack. The closed curtains fluttered lightly in the night breeze.

Delicious anticipation fluttered in her stomach as he turned back to her in the soft amber glow of the table lamp and tugged her into his arms, his mouth groping for hers, finding it, sucking gently on her lower lip and caressing it softly with his tongue.

His fingers slipped beneath the fall of her hair to find the zip of her dress and he pulled it slowly down in one smooth motion, sliding the fluttering sleeves from her shoulders, his mouth tracing the blade of her collarbone with tiny kisses. He smoothed her dress lower, until it fell from her body into a gleaming puddle of silk on the floor. And then her mind followed his hands as they explored her body, as he unhooked her bra, cast it aside and cupped her breasts softly in his palms. Her nipples were pinched lightly between his fingers, sending dizzying flutters down her spine where they intensified hotly between her legs.

Then came brief unsteadiness as he slid his hands firmly beneath her thighs and lifted her against him. She could feel his rigid arousal press against her as she curled her legs around his waist and he carried her the few paces across the room to the antique desk. He held her tightly against him and she leaned sideways as he swept her belongings carelessly onto the floor. Body lotion and hairbrush fell with meaningless thuds onto the deep-pile carpet, and then there was cool, smooth wood against her skin as he put her down on the desk in just her panties.

She'd had a few boyfriends, yes. In the dim and distant past she'd done the rounds, albeit in a minor way, at university. None of it had felt like this. And if during the last year she'd let herself imagine what it might feel like to be with him it had never touched this reality. His every touch made her heart leap and her stomach flutter. His touch was expert, but there was nothing by rote about this. He seemed in tune with her every need and desire, as if he could read her mind.

His hands found her thighs again, parting them softly, and then he was tracing kisses down her neck, his mouth sliding lower until he closed his lips over her nipple, teasing it softly with his tongue. Heat simmered in her stomach and pooled meltingly between her thighs as he sank to his knees and traced his mouth lightly over the flat of her stomach. She sucked in a sharp breath as his lips sank lower still and the heat of his breath warmed her through the lace of her panties. She gasped as his fingers teased the thin fabric aside and his tongue slipped against the very core of her.

Her hands found his hair and clutched at it as he stroked and teased until she ached for him to go further, and then delicious pleasure flooded her veins as he slid two fingers inside her in one slow and smooth movement. She moaned softly as he found his rhythm, moving his fingers steadily as his tongue lazily circled the nub of her, moving with her, until she cried her ecstasy at the ceiling and he moved both hands beneath her, holding her against his mouth, wringing every last second of satisfaction out of her.

Anonymity was gone. That inconsequential, easy gratification wasn't there. Because for once this wasn't about quick fun, satisfaction. Dispensable satisfaction.

This was about her. Wanting to please *her*. And that was a real novelty that knocked his senses sprawling.

The light change in her breath as he ran his fingertips over the softness of her thighs, the way she gasped and clutched at his hair as he moved them higher—all those little gestures delighted him and turned him on all the more.

Dan got to his feet in the hollow between her parted legs and pulled her close. She curled her arms around him, tugging him against her, her fast, short breaths warm against his lips. Her evident excitement, such a foil to her usual carefully controlled attitude, thrilled him to the core, and in the all-encompassing heat of his arousal he marvelled at the surge of excitement pleasing her elicited.

He had been going through the motions all this time. His dates, his easy flings… Plenty of them, but all a simple good time means to an end. The cost of that had been the detached quality about them that meant pleasure had failed to touch him below the physical surface. The combination of his visceral hot need for Emma, his delight at her eagerness to please him and his own desire to please her took him way beyond that level. There was nothing run of the mill about this.

The thought crept through his mind, tinged with fear at the deeper meaning of it, but he moved on regardless, powerless to stop.

He lifted her, his hands sliding across the cool satiny skin of her lower back, the sweet vanilla scent of her hair dizzying his senses, and crushed his mouth hard against hers. His desire for her was rising inside him like a cresting wave, driving him forward. Her legs wrapped around his waist as he carried her the few paces from desk to four-poster and eased her down gently onto the softness of the quilted bedspread.

And now he moved with intimate slowness, the better to savour every second, to explore. She slid gentle hands over his back and sparks of arousal jumped and flickered in his abdomen as her fingers found his hard length and stroked with deliciously maddening softness. A guttural moan escaped his lips as he tangled a hand in the silk of her hair and crushed his mouth against hers, easing her lips apart with his tongue.

Before he could be consumed by the deliciousness of it he caught her hand and moved away briefly to find a condom. And then control was his again as he moved against her, and her gasp thrilled him as he eased slowly into her. As she raised her hips with a soft moan, urging him on, sliding her hands around him to push him deeper into her, greedy for more, his spirits soared. And only as she clutched at his back and cried her pleasure against his neck did he finally let himself follow her over that delicious edge.

Bewildering *déjà vu* kicked in as Emma woke to birdsong and sunshine for the second time in a weekend. And then all thoughts of her surroundings disappeared as she came fully awake in one crushing instant of consciousness. She turned her head slowly on the pillow.

Not a hallucination brought on by wedding stress and too much champagne.

Dan was in the bed next to her. And they'd spent the night exploring every inch of one another. Hell, her cheeks fired just at the thought of what they'd done and she pressed her face against the cool top sheet. Had that *really* been her? Super-cool, professional Emma? Brazen—that was what she was.

His dark hair was dishevelled even beyond its usual spikes by action and sleep, and there was a light shadow of stubble now defining his jaw. She lifted a hand to her dry mouth as her gaze ranged down the defined muscles of his torso to the sheet that lay haphazardly over his hips. He was the stuff of dreams.

But the cold light of day was streaming in right through that window. She'd joined the ranks of Dan's little-black-book girls. How long did he usually leave it before he did his backing off? A day? Two?

She held her breath and without sitting up began wriggling inch by slow inch towards the edge of the bed, not really thinking much further at this point than getting some clothes on. They might have spent half the night screwing, but that didn't mean he'd have the chance to ogle her cellulite in daylight.

She was right on the edge of the bed and just thinking

about how to manoeuvre her feet onto the floor when he took a deep, relaxed breath and opened his eyes.

She froze like a rabbit in headlights.

'You look surprised,' he said, stretching easily.

He gave her that slow, laconic grin that never failed to make her stomach do flip-flops. Clearly she had the *look* of a rabbit in headlights, too.

'Is it such a disappointment to wake up next to me?'

She clutched the top of the sheet a modest few inches above nipple height and tried to move her bum cheeks back fully onto the bed so he wouldn't realise she'd been trying to make an exit.

'I wasn't sure I would,' she said. 'I half expected you to make a swift exit under cover of darkness. Didn't you tell me that was your usual modus operandi? Not to make it through to breakfast?'

He pulled himself up onto one elbow and smiled down at her. The benefit of having hair that naturally spiked was that he actually looked *better* first thing in the morning. How typical. She could just imagine the fright wig on her own head after the active night they'd spent.

'Emma, nothing about this is my usual modus operandi.'

His blue eyes held her own and her stomach gave a slow and toe-curling flip as the delectable things he'd done to her last night danced through her mind. He reached a hand out to stroke her cheek softly and a surge of happiness began to bubble through her. He was right. None of this fitted with him acting to type. Yet still it was hard to let herself trust him.

'I know you too well,' she said. 'That's the thing. None of your usual lines will work on me.'

'I wasn't aware I'd used any,' he said.

He had a point. He'd bailed her brother out, he hadn't washed his hands of her and disappeared to London after she'd called him selfish, he'd carried himself brilliantly through her brother's crazy wedding and he was still here at breakfast time. She let her guard slip.

Self-doubt. Any other reaction from her would be a surprise, wouldn't it?

Just looking at her lying next to him, all long limbs and messy hair and uncertainty, made heat begin to simmer again deep inside him. The night they'd spent replayed in his mind on a loop—the way she'd slowly put her trust in him, shedding her inhibitions, giving as much as taking. He wanted to smooth every kink of doubt out of her, convince her that this was far more than the throwaway night she clearly thought it might be.

He reached across and pulled her into his arms, fitting her long, slender body against his own, breathing in the faint sweet vanilla scent that still clung to her hair. His mouth found hers and he parted her lips hungrily with his tongue and kissed her deeply.

Desire rippled through her, peaking at her nipples and pooling between her legs as he gently turned her over, his mouth at her shoulder.

In her dreams of all those months ago he had been skilled. In reality he was melt-to-the-floor perfect. How did he know how to make her feel that sublime? Where to touch her? How hard to stroke? How softly to caress?

He lay behind her now, her pleasure his sole focus. One hand was circling her waist, his fingers easing slowly between her thighs, softly parting them to expose the core of her. She felt his moan of satisfaction against her neck as he discovered how wet she was. His thumb found her most sensitive spot and circled it with tantalising slowness. His fingers slid lower, teasing until she ached with emptiness and desire.

And then he was turning her expertly, one hand pressed flat beneath her stomach, the other cradling her breasts as he moved behind her. A moment of delicious anticipation as he paused to grab a condom, then she felt him press against her. And then he was thrusting smoothly deep inside her, filling her deliciously, his free hand teasing her nipples to rock-hard points, his mouth at her neck. As she cried out in uncontrolled pleasure he moaned his own ecstasy against the smooth contours of her back, not slowing or changing pace until he knew she was satisfied.

Afterwards, she lay in his arms, the warm length of his torso against her back, his soft breath against her hair. His hand circled her body, lightly cupping her breast, caressing it. They fitted together perfectly, as if they were meant to be together. For the first time she let herself tentatively believe that they might be. He'd made love to her again instead of making a sharp exit. He was still here with her. Yet still there were things that needed to be said.

'I didn't say thank you, did I?' she said softly. When he didn't answer she turned her head slightly, to catch his expression at her shoulder. 'For restoring Adam's shadow for me.'

She felt him tense briefly, then he tugged gently at her shoulder until she turned over in his arms and lay facing him. His mouth was inches from her own and his gaze was holding hers steadily.

He looked at her resigned expression and mentally kicked himself.

'I didn't mean that,' he said. 'It was a crappy thing to say. I know how difficult your family can be.' He paused as if groping for the right words. 'It wasn't a personal dig at you. It was more about reacting to your telling me where to get off.'

'You always have to have the last word,' she said quietly. 'I've noticed that about you. Why is that? Why is it so hard for you to accept anyone else's agenda? People *do* have them, you know—it's not just *you* living in a bubble.'

Was that how she really saw him? Was he really that blind to other people's feelings?

'It wasn't intentional,' he said. 'I'm sorry if it seemed that way to you. It was…' He groped for a way to explain that wouldn't sound totally crap. 'I like staying in control,' he said at last. 'Being the one that makes all the decisions. Perhaps it's become a bit of a habit.' He paused and added, 'A defence mechanism.'

The same one he'd used so successfully since childhood.

'If the only person you look out for is yourself, you can't be hurt.'

'I don't understand.'

He looked at the ceiling, at the blank white expanse of it.

'There was someone once,' he said. 'I'm not talking about one of the girls I see now. They're just dates. Nothing more to it than that. There was someone else a long time ago.'

He didn't look at her. It felt easier, not doing that.

'Maggie and I were housemates at college,' he said.

'There were six of us. Couple of girls, four blokes, each of us renting a room and sharing a kitchen and bathroom. You know the kind of thing. Student accommodation. For the first time I was living away from home.'

He remembered how liberating it had felt that his life was finally his own. An escape route.

'We were friends, Maggie and me, then one night after a party we ended up sleeping together. We kept it really casual, though. Both of us had big career plans. She was training to be a teacher. Primary school kids, you know?'

He glanced at Emma and she nodded acknowledgment, not interrupting. That was a good thing. If he stopped talking about this now he might never start again.

'And she lived up north, had a big family there, and she was going to be moving back once she'd finished her course. It wasn't serious. It was never *going* to be serious.' He laughed. 'Hell, I'd just got *away* from home life, finally tasted a bit of freedom. I wasn't about to get myself tied down to someone before I'd even finished my first year.'

She looked puzzled.

'But you did? You must have for her to have made such a big impact on you. What happened?'

He paused, gathering his thoughts. Who had he told about the baby? Anyone at all? He stormed ahead before he could think twice.

'Maggie got pregnant,' he said simply.

He felt the change in her posture as she shifted in his arms. She lifted herself on one elbow to look at him. He steeled himself to glance at her and read the response

in her face, ready for the questions that he was sure
would follow.

She said nothing. Her eyes were filled with gentle-
ness but she didn't speak, didn't pry. She was letting him
talk on his own terms.

'And that changed everything,' he said.

He took a sharp breath as he recalled the memory. It
came back to him easily, in such perfect clarity that it
made a mockery of his conviction that he'd done such a
great job of putting it behind him.

'At first I was horrified. I thought it was the last thing
I could possibly want. Maggie had strong views. She was
going to keep the baby whether I was involved or not.'
He sighed. 'She made it sound like she was offering me
my freedom, but looking back I think to her I was dispensable even at the outset.'

'And were you? Involved, I mean?'

He could see the puzzlement in her eyes. She was
wondering if he had a secret family stashed away somewhere.

'Once I got used to the shock I was more and more
delighted. The longer it went on the more I bought into
it. With every day that passed I had a clearer idea of
what the future would be like. I was going to be the best
bloody husband and father the world had ever seen.'

'You've been married?'

He gave a rueful smile and shook his head.

'It was my one and only brush with it, but, no, it never
happened. I wanted it to be as different to my experi-
ence of family as I could make it. Proper commitment,
hands-on parents with a strong, healthy relationship.'
He paused. 'I probably envisaged a white picket fence
somewhere. And a dog. Sunday roasts. All the stereo-

types. I was right in there with them.' He took a breath. 'And then it all disappeared overnight because we lost the baby.'

The wrenching, churning ache deep in his chest made a suffocating comeback. Dulled a little at the edges over time, like an old wound, but still there, still heavy.

She was sitting up now, reaching for his hands, her eyes filled with sadness.

'Oh, bloody hell, Dan. I'm so sorry.'

He waved a dismissive hand at her, shaking his head, swallowing hard to rid his throat of the aching constriction.

'It was a long time ago,' he said.

In terms of years, at least.

'I'm over it.'

'I never imagined you being remotely interested in kids or family,' she said. 'I mean, it isn't just the way you keep your relationships so short or the fact you never see your own parents. You're the most un-child-friendly person I've ever known. You have a penthouse flat with a balcony and it's full of glass furniture and white up-holstery. Your car is a two-seater.'

'Why would I need a family home or a Volvo?' he said. 'I have absolutely no intention of going down that road again. I gave it my best shot and it didn't work out.'

A worried frown played about her face and he gave her a reassuring *I'm-over-it* smile.

'That's why I didn't step straight up to the plate when Adam needed a helping hand. That's why I made it into the car before I realised I couldn't leave for London. I was trying to play things the way I always do. I don't get involved with people. I like keeping things simple.'

'At arm's length.'

'Exactly. Arm's length. After Maggie I decided relationships weren't for me. Family wasn't for me. I threw
myself into work instead. After all, it had always worked
at digging me out in the past. And it worked again.'
He shrugged. 'But maybe it's become a bit of a habit. I
never wanted to come across as selfish or unkind when
I said you liked your comfort zone. It was a retaliation,
nothing more.'

He pulled her back down from her elbow into a cud-
dle. Her head nestled beneath his chin. She shook her
head slowly against his chest.

'Maybe it *was* just a retaliation but actually you might
have had a point,' she said quietly.

He pulled away enough to give her a questioning look
and she offered him a tiny smile.

'A *small* point,' she qualified. 'Did you ever know I
had a crush on you for months, like some stupid school-
girl?'

That flash of clarity kicked in again, the same as he'd
felt the night before, as if something he wasn't seeing
had been pointed out to him. A wood instead of a mass
of trees, maybe.

'You did?'

'Why am I not surprised that you never noticed?'
She sighed and rolled her eyes. 'I think maybe part of
the reason I was so struck on you was because of what
you're like. I knew you'd never look twice at me. I didn't
fit your remit.'

'My *remit?*' He grinned and tugged her closer.

She snuggled into his arm. 'Blonde, bubbly, curva-
ceous. That's your type.'

'Dispensable, simplistic, inconsequential,' he said.

'Those were the real qualities I was aiming for. None of which apply to you.'

'That's exactly my point. I got to know you over months, I saw the kind of girls you went for and I knew none of your relationships lasted. I knew you'd never be interested in me and that made dreaming about the prospect from afar a very nice, safe thing to do.'

She held a hand up as if it was all suddenly clear to her.

'Plus it was a great reason not to get involved with anyone else, and it gave me the perfect way to fob off criticism from my parents when they asked about my life. So there you are, you see. When you said I was happy living in Adam's shadow, staying under my parents' radar, you kind of had a point. My choices were all about keeping an easy life.'

'You must have hidden it well,' he said, scanning his mind back over the last twelve months. Little signs jumped out at him now that he had that hindsight—the way she'd always been available for any work engagement, no matter how short the notice, the effort she'd always made with her appearance. He'd assumed those were things she did for everyone. Because that was what he'd *wanted* to assume. The alternative hadn't been allowed on his radar.

'Then again, I'm not sure I would have noticed unless you'd smashed me over the head with it,' he conceded. 'I had you filed very comfortably under "Work Colleague". That was what I needed you to be. I never intended things between us to be more than that.'

'Our plus-one agreement.'

He didn't respond, although the ensuing silence was heavy with the unspoken question. What would happen now with their ludicrous arrangement? He'd told her it would be over when they got this weekend out of the way and went back to their London lives. With every moment he spent with her, sticking to that decision and riding it out felt more and more difficult.

CHAPTER ELEVEN

'You want to try and get to breakfast?' he asked.

Emma felt the light brush of his kiss against her shoulder. Even after the night they'd spent, followed by the delicious intimacy of this morning, his touch thrilled her.

She wriggled against him. Her arms fitted around his neck as if they were meant to be there. She smoothed the dense spikes of his hair through her fingers.

'Let me think,' she said, smiling into his eyes. 'Would I rather sit opposite my parents and watch my father drool over a full English while my mother force-feeds him muesli, or would I rather stay here with you?'

He laughed and pulled her tighter.

'Adam's married now. I think he's grown-up enough to manage without me watching his back through one little breakfast.' She dropped her eyes briefly. 'And I think you've done enough for him. We can catch him before he goes.'

Was it just that? Or was part of it that she didn't want to leave this gorgeous little bubble where he was hers for fear that it might burst? After wanting him for so long, all the while convinced nothing would ever come of it, to actually have her crush requited made it seem all the sweeter.

Needling doubt lurked at the edge of her consciousness despite the gorgeous night they'd spent and the way he'd opened up about his past. She knew Dan—knew the way he played relationships. Despite his reassurances there was no getting away from the fact that pretty soon after you made it into Dan's bed you made it just as quickly out of it, never to be heard of again. Was this like some holiday romance? Would the magic be theirs as long as they didn't leave? What would happen when they got back to London?

She'd noticed that her mention of the old plus-one agreement hadn't been picked up by him. His intention to cut all ties with her after this weekend gnawed at the edge of her consciousness as she tried to push it away.

Adam and Ernie stood at the hotel doorway, waving madly. Those who had made it down to breakfast clustered in the lobby. Emma had dragged Dan downstairs with moments to spare and eased her way through the group of smiling friends and relatives, her hand entwined in his.

Emma's mother dabbed a tear from the corner of her eye.

'Well, it wasn't the most traditional set-up,' she sniffed, 'but still…it's been a lovely weekend.'

She kissed Adam's cheek and then leaned in to do the same to Ernie.

'Tradition?' Ernie said. 'I think we can stretch to a bit of that before we go.'

He grabbed at a bunch of yellow lilies standing in a huge vase on the side table near the door, turned his back on the gathered crowd of guests and lobbed them high in the air over his head to the sound of claps and squeals, showering the guests with drops of water. As the flowers plummeted, twisting and turning, faces turned to watch their progress.

Dan shot out a hand and caught them on autopilot, to prevent them from smacking him over the head.

He stared down stupidly at the bunch of flowers in his hand as cheers and mad clapping rang out all around them. Even Emma's mother was smiling.

'You're next!' Adam hollered from the doorway. 'Great catch, sweetie!'

Dan glanced at Emma and saw the look of delight on her face. Her eyes shone. Her smile lit up her face. She radiated happiness.

Shock flooded into the pit of his stomach.

You're next!

Was he? Was that where this led?

He'd had a game plan way back in London, before they'd even set foot in the West Country. A plan to be a last-time-pays-for-all fake boyfriend stand-in for Emma and then go back to London. Back to work. Back to what *worked*. And somehow he'd been caught up in the moment, had lost sight of what was important to him.

He'd ended up standing here with flowers in his hands to the sound of excited applause because the path ahead of him led down the aisle. Maybe not now, maybe not even in the next few years, but *that* was the destination.

If they made it that far.

That was the risk. A risk he'd vowed never to take again after the months of despair that had plagued him when Maggie left.

This was way off-plan. Yet the thought of losing Emma now made his heart plummet and misery churn in his stomach.

He followed the rest of the group outside to watch Adam and Ernie pile into a yellow Rolls-Royce. Maybe he could find another way forward. A way to keep her that still minimised risk. A compromise.

She'd been right.

There really was more between them than one of his casual flings. They'd been back from the wedding for nearly a week now and he was a different man. He was in touch with her daily, and with every phone call and text she felt more secure. Flowers arrived from him at her workplace, eliciting envious stares and buzzing interest from her colleagues. He hadn't so much as mentioned their old plus-one agreement, but that was because it was obsolete—right? Past history. OK, so she wasn't expecting him to propose…let's not get ahead of ourselves—although a girl could dream. But she'd been the one to change his behaviour. He really *was* different with her. They were a couple now—not just work contacts.

Dan didn't *do* flowers and phone calls. He did swift exits and dumping by text. And now she was seeing him tonight and her stomach was one big ball of excitement and anticipation. She couldn't wait.

The doorbell. On time.

She checked her appearance one last time. A new dress, a less austere one than usual, with a floaty, feminine skirt. Deep pink instead of her usual black or grey choice of going-out outfit. Because going out with Dan was about pleasure now, not business. About getting to know each other instead of working the situation for every career advantage they could get out of it.

She opened the front door and excitement at seeing him brought an instant smile to her face—one she couldn't have held back. He stood on the doorstep, leaning against the jamb, his crisp blue shirt deepening the tones of his eyes as he smiled at her, a perfectly cut business suit and silk tie sharpening the look.

Not the same relaxed designer look he'd had at the wedding weekend. Her mind stuttered briefly. *Business suit*.

From nowhere cautionary unease jabbed her in the ribs and a wave of disorientating *déjà vu* swept over her. She could have rewound to a couple of months before Adam's wedding, before Alistair had put a stop to their agreement, and Dan would have looked exactly like this when she'd opened the door for one of their business engagements.

He slid an arm around her waist and kissed her softly on the mouth, starting up all the latent sparks from the weekend.

She pulled herself up short.

Jumping at shadows—that was what she was doing. She was so used to being doomed to failure when she put herself out there that now she was pre-empting problems before they even happened. She'd ruin things herself if she wasn't careful. Already he had a puzzled expression on his face—no doubt because her first reaction on seeing him since their gorgeous weekend at the wedding was to hesitate.

He'd called her. He'd sent flowers. He'd texted. And now she was spooked because of the *suit* he wore? She really needed to go to work on her own insecurities if she was going to move forward with her life.

'Where are we going, then?' she asked when he started the car.

'Dinner first,' he said easily, putting it in gear and

moving smoothly into the early-evening traffic. 'I've got a table booked at La Maison.'

Another jab of unease.

'La Maison?'

It was Dan's choice of venue for work dinners. She'd been there with him too many times to count, always as his stand-in date, always with a work objective in mind. Maybe it would be a new contact to impress, perhaps a sweetener before he put in a tender for services. Whatever it happened to be, she'd been there to help smooth the path.

He glanced across at her.

'For starters, yes. If that's OK with you? Then maybe later we could go on somewhere else? End up at my place?'

'Of course.'

She smiled brightly at him and pressed her palms together in her lap. They were damp.

He parked the car and escorted her into the restaurant. The usual subtle piano music played in the background, and the usual perfectly dressed dark wood tables and soft lighting provided the perfect ambience for discussion, which had always been the point of coming here.

His usual table. She felt Dan's hand rest gently on her hip as he guided her between the tables towards it.

Usual restaurant. Usual table.

It didn't mean anything, did it? The restaurant was a good one after all.

Usual quick run-through of background?

'Roger Lewis and Barry Trent,' he said in a low voice at her shoulder. 'Medium-sized business providing bespoke travel packages specifically aimed at the over-fifties. Looking for advice on growing their business to the next level.' He gave her shoulder a squeeze. 'Could be in the market for a change in legal services, too—you could be in there!'

As they arrived at the table she turned to stare at him and he actually *winked* at her. It felt as if her heart was being squeezed in a vice.

'Table for four,' she said dully, stating the obvious.

He looked at her as if she might be mad. As if there was nothing spot-the-deliberate-mistake about this at all.

'Of course it is,' he said. 'Just a bit of business to discuss and then the evening's ours. They'll be along in a minute.'

The waiter pulled a chair out for her and fussed over her as she sat down hard, her mind reeling. Dan gave him the nod and he poured them each a glass of champagne, replacing the bottle in the ice bucket to one side of the table.

Her throat felt as if it might be closing up and she swallowed hard. She clasped her hands together on the table to stop them shaking.

'I thought we were going on a date,' she said, making her tone as neutral as she could manage when what she wanted to do was grab him by the shoulders and shake him. 'Just you and me. But this is basically the same old set-up, Dan.'

She waved a hand at the extra two table settings, at the surrounding quiet tastefulness of the restaurant.

'Is that it, then? Now we're back in London it's back to the same old routine? Were you actually going to discuss that with me, or did you just assume I'd go along with it?'

He reached for her hands but she removed them to her lap.

'I don't know what you mean,' he said.

'What this looks like to me is the same old plus-one agreement,' she said, forcing the words out, voicing her worst fears. 'Just with sex thrown in.'

He grimaced and leaned across the table to touch her cheek.

'This is *not* the same old plus-one agreement,' he said, 'and I really wish we'd never given the damn thing a name. It makes it sound like we signed something official when all we really did was get into a routine over time. Because it worked so well for *both* of us.'

A routine? She pressed her lips together hard and pushed a hand through her hair as anger began to course through her. It felt suddenly uncomfortably hot in here. She hadn't missed the emphasis there on the word *both*. No way was she letting him lump her in with this as if it were some joint bloody venture.

When he next spoke it felt as if he'd tipped the contents of the ice bucket over her head.

'But if we *have* to call it that,' he continued, holding out a hand, 'for what it's worth I don't think we should be too hasty about changing how we relate to each other when it comes to work. Why end something that's worked so well for us just because you and I have got closer? What do you think about varying it a little? Adding in a few amendments?'

His tone was jokey—teasing, even. As if he were proposing something exciting. As if she ought to be taking his arm off in her eagerness to say yes.

'Different rules this time—it'll be fun. We can still do work engagements together, give it everything we've got just like we always have, but without the need to limit it. There'll be no need to *pretend* we're a couple any more—no need to go our separate ways at the end of the night.'

He wanted to carry on seeing her but without any full-on legitimacy. Work would continue to come first with him, just the way it always had. He would expect her to carry on acting as his plus-one, smoothing the way for his business prowess at charity dinners and the like. The difference would be that this time she would get to share his bed, as well.

Well, *lucky, lucky* her.

All the pent-up excitement that had built this week as she'd looked forward to seeing him again had quit bubbling and dissipated like flat champagne. The flavour would still be there—the tang of white grape and the sharp aroma reminiscent of the effervescent drink it once was—but when you got right down to it, it was past its best. What you were really getting was the dregs.

And one thing she knew without a shadow of a doubt was that she was not going to be the dregs. Not for anyone.

Not even for him.

She stood up, a veil of calm slipping over her. She'd wanted him to be hers so much she'd believed she'd give anything to keep him.

But when it came to it she found that her self-respect just wasn't up for grabs.

He looked up at her, his expression confused, as she picked up her handbag and lifted her wrap from the back of her chair, making it obvious this wasn't just a visit to the ladies' room. She was leaving.

'Where are you going?'

'Home,' she said, not looking at him.

She pushed her chair back into place. Sick disappointment burned in her throat, blocking it. She wasn't sure she could stop it transforming into tears if she looked at him. She absolutely was *not* going to cry. No way.

He stood up immediately, his hand on her elbow.

'Why? What's wrong? Are you ill?'

The look of concern in his eyes touched her heart and she almost faltered. But this was just too bloody reminiscent of the last guy she'd met for dinner, thinking she was on her way to a happy ending. Dan was just like Alistair after all.

'No, Dan,' she said. 'I'm not ill. I'm stupid. Stupid for thinking there might actually be more between us than *work.*'

She made a move to leave and he grabbed her by the hand.

'Hey, we can talk about this. That's what this is about? You're annoyed because I factored a work dinner into our date night?' He shrugged. 'I'm sorry. Maybe I should have talked to you about it first. I just didn't think you'd mind. Before last weekend you were all for carrying on with the agreement, and you'd gone back to work instead of taking that sabbatical, so I just assumed you'd be all for it.'

'That was before the weekend,' she said.

She looked down at her hand, encased in his.

'This isn't what I want. Some half-arsed excuse for a relationship. I thought you understood that. I don't want some relationship where we both have our own agenda and factor the other person in wherever they happen to fit. You know where that kind of relationship ends up?' She didn't wait for his answer. 'It ends up with separate bedrooms and separate interests and separate bloody lives. If we can't even get that right now, what hope do we have? I want you and me to be the priority—not an afterthought to whatever work ambitions we might happen to have.'

'It never bothered you before,' he pointed out.

'Because it was all I *had* before,' she said. 'It was the only way I could have some level of relationship with you. But I want more than that now. And after last weekend I thought you wanted that, too.'

Two business-suited middle-aged men were being ushered between the tables towards them. The over-fifties leisure break people, she assumed.

'Don't go,' he said. 'Let's get this business discussion out of the way and then we can talk this through properly.'

She gave a wry laugh and flung her hands up.

'That's the problem, you see. Right there. You *still* think I might actually sit down and put your work meeting first—before we get to talk about what's happening between us. I'm not doing it. Whatever this is for you—plus-one bloody agreement, quick fling, friends with benefits—it's over.'

She'd raised her voice and some of the diners seated nearby rubbernecked to stare at them. She didn't give a damn. She had no intention of ever visiting this restaurant again. In fact, the way she felt right now, she might not go out socially again. Possibly ever. Maybe she'd embrace her inner workaholic and make senior partnership by thirty-five. A new goal. One that was attainable. One that relied solely on her and so wasn't doomed to failure.

She walked away from the table.

He moved after her as she passed the two businessmen, one with his hand outstretched. She heard Dan apologise briefly before he ran after her. He caught her near the door, took her arm, turned her to face him.

'You're dumping me?' A grin lifted the corner of his mouth.

Her heart twisted agonisingly in her chest.

'Yes,' she said.

'What? No champagne-throwing?' he joked, as if he still couldn't believe she was making such a fuss.

She didn't smile. It felt as if her veins were full of ice water.

'That was a *fake* break-up, Dan,' she said. 'All for show. This is the real thing.'

She walked out of the restaurant without looking back.

CHAPTER TWELVE

DAN STARED AT the city skyline from the balcony of his flat. Grey today, misted in drizzle. The fine rain was the kind that coated and his hair and skin were slowly soaking; the boards were slick beneath his feet.

So she'd dumped him.

No one dumped him. *Ever.* And now she'd done it twice in the space of a couple of months.

The confused feeling of a loss of control which had buried him the first time, back at the art gallery, kicked right back into action. Had that really only been a month or two ago? It felt like years.

He wasn't going to make the same mistake again—grappling for control of the situation and leaving himself open to a second body blow.

Except it really hadn't been just a body blow, had it? *Let it go.*

In the first defiant moments after she'd left him to sort out the embarrassment in the restaurant that had felt doable. He didn't need this kind of chaos in his life. That had been the whole point of keeping relationships distant. He'd had a lucky escape.

In the ensuing days it had become more and more difficult to keep himself convinced of that. It wasn't as if he'd let her have an access-all-areas pass to his life after all. Their paths crossed at work functions, they communicated via e-mail and the occasional phone call. Businesslike. At arm's length. She'd visited his flat on two or three occasions—never when it was just the two of them. So it wasn't as if her absence left a gaping hole in his life where she'd previously been. How could you miss something that you never had?

He knew that was possible better than anyone.

Somewhere in the depths of his consciousness he understood that what he was missing was the way she'd made him feel—the way she'd altered his take on life.

He'd spent so long making sure no one became important to him, but she'd somehow managed to get past that barrier. She'd done it so quietly that he hadn't realised how much he needed her until she was gone, so perfect had his conviction been that he had everything under control.

It had seemed like the perfect solution—the perfect way to keep things at the comfortable distance he'd thought he needed. Why not just reinstate the old social agreement? Keep their relationship grounded in something that was tried and tested? Keep some areas of his life untouched rather than investing his entire soul in something that might fail?

And in his stupid arrogance he'd just expected her to go along with his every whim, just to accept that their relationship had a work slant to it. Especially after her revelation about her age-old crush on him. She'd taken whatever he'd thrown her way for the last year, never asking for anything in return, and he saw now that he'd just taken that for granted.

If anything he admired her all the more for finally

standing up for what she wanted. She'd wanted out because she wasn't prepared to settle for second best. After years of playing second fiddle to Adam and then being trounced by that moron Alistair Woods she'd been ready to risk everything to be with him and he'd failed her. He'd been too afraid to reciprocate.

The flat that she'd barely visited now felt empty where it had always felt relaxing. So far removed from any family vibe, he'd been able to look around him and know he'd built a new life—one that was successful, one that couldn't collapse under emotional rubble. The prospect of living here now felt empty. He'd had a taste of a different life. He'd tried to keep it in check. But apparently a taste was all that was needed to suck him totally in.

He was in love with her. And it was too late now to guard against loss because the damage was done. He'd screwed up.

He glanced around the balcony—hot tub with its cover on in the corner, railings with a sheer drop below. What had she said—his life was child-unfriendly? It was. Deliberately so. Only now he began to question whether he still wanted that. Whether he ever truly had.

He moved back inside and slid the double doors shut. The flat was totally silent and devoid of character. No mess. No clutter.

He could let this go. See if he couldn't put it behind him. Hell, work had done the trick before—it might do it again. Perhaps if he ceased eating and sleeping and all other essential functions, doubled the effort with his business, he could crush her from his mind.

Or he could take a risk.

He glanced around him again. What, really, did he have to lose?

* * *

'…and Adam and Ernie are heading back from Mauritius. Adam's already got a ton of interest in his new planned collection of pictures and there's talk of them being immortalised on table mats and coasters. Can you imagine?' Her mother paused a moment to let the enormity of that fact sink in. 'That's the kind of mass appeal he has.'

Emma held the phone briefly away from her ear. Dan should have held out for a share in Adam's business in return for helping him. He could have made a mint. Then again, it would have been another tie, another responsibility, another link to a family he wanted to keep at a distance. Of course he wouldn't have wanted that.

She gritted her teeth hard and forced Dan out of her mind, to which he seemed to return at the slightest opportunity.

She put the phone back to her ear.

'What about you? Any news?' her mother was saying. 'Is that Dan showing any signs of making an honest woman of you?' She gave the briefest of pauses, clearly believing the answer was a foregone conclusion of a no. 'Thought not. Work, then?'

How many times had Emma had varying versions of this same conversation? Made the right noises just to avoid interest and interference, just to keep her comfort zone comfortable? She never had any new successes to hold up to her mother's scrutiny, but she never had any epic failures, either. Comfortable, uncomplicated middle ground. And where exactly had it got her?

She opened her mouth to give her mother some stock fob-off—something that would buy her another couple of months below the radar before she had to repeat this whole stupid fake conversation all over again. Probably it would be something about her legal career boring enough to have her mother fast-forwarding onto her next gossip morsel before she could scrutinise Emma's life beyond the surface. It had worked like a dream these last few years.

For the first time in millions of conversations she hesitated.

She was the most miserable she could ever remember being and the hideous pain was sharpened to gut-wrenching level because she'd known that brief spell of sublime perfection before Dan had reverted to type. In actual fact there had been no reversion. He'd never left type. It had all been a façade.

Was there *any* aspect of her life left that was real or of value?

'Dan and I aren't together,' she blurted, then clapped a hand over her own mouth in shock at her own words. 'We never were.'

Except for a week or two when I thought I was the stand-out one who could change him.

'We work together and we had an agreement to stand in as each other's dates at parties and dinners.'

For the first time ever there was stunned silence on the end of the phone and Emma had the oddest sensation in her stomach. A surge of off-the-wall indignant defiance. She picked it up and ran with it.

She really had been wallowing in the role of Adam's underachieving sibling all these years, kidding herself about how hard that was, when in reality it had been the easy option. Pigeonholing herself as failure meant she had absolutely nothing to live up to.

She didn't need to define herself by her childhood inadequacies—she had known that for years—but knowing it really wasn't enough. The real issue was whether or not she'd truly bought into that. Or had a part of her remained that sweaty-palmed kid on the stage in spite of the passing years?

For the first time she took a breath and really did buy into it. Just how much of her inadequacy was she responsible for? Who had put Adam on a gilded pedestal and kept him there? Guilty as charged. It had been easier to live in his shadow than to prove herself in her own right.

Had it in some way been easier to accept the categorisation of herself as the clumsy one? The underachiever? The let-down? The singleton? No relationships for her, because that would lead to rejection. Just oodles of work, because that was the one thing she could feel good at, because it depended only on her. Had it been easier to blame her family for her failures instead of living an actual functional, healthy life?

'I'm taking a sabbatical from work,' she said. 'I'm going travelling.'

All that excitement she'd had about going away with Alistair, about escaping her dreary old life where everything was safe and secure and devoid of risk, made a cautious comeback. When she'd finished with him she'd finished with all of that, too. But now that Adam's wedding was over and the train wreck that was her friendship, relationship, romance with Dan was finished—she wasn't even sure what the bloody hell to call it—what exactly was there to keep her here? Why the hell did she need Alistair on her arm to have an adventure of her own?

She had absolutely no idea what she wanted in life any more, so why not take the time to find out?

* * *

She slid her bag from her shoulder and sat down at a pavement café overlooking the harbour. She ordered coffee and watched the bustle of tourists passing by, queuing for boat trips, browsing the local shops, fishing. The sun warmed her shoulders in the simple linen dress she wore. Just time for a coffee before her own boat trip departed—a day cruise around the island.

She looked up as someone snagged the seat opposite her with their foot, and her heart leapt as they pulled it out and sat down.

She must be seeing things. Maybe that was what happened when you missed someone enough—no matter how stupid and pointless missing them might be.

He took his sunglasses off and smiled at her, and she knew instantly that for all her telling herself she was way over him her thundering heart had the real measure of things.

'How did you find me?' she said.

He motioned to the waiter, ordered coffee.

'I had to ask your mother.'

Damn, he'd been serious about tracking her down, then.

'And how did that work for you?' She kept her voice carefully neutral.

'Well, it was no picnic, I can tell you.'

'She doesn't know where I'm staying,' she said. 'I've been picking up accommodation as I go along, depending where I want to go next.'

'I know. Didn't sound like you. What—no agenda? No travel itinerary?'

She grinned at that. At how well he knew her.

'My life's been one massive agenda these last few

years—all about what impression I want to give to this person or that person. I needed a change. My mistake was waiting for someone else to come along and instigate that instead of biting the bullet myself.'

'She told me you'd been e-mailing her, and she knew you'd booked a boat trip from here today. She just didn't know what time.'

She stared at him.

'You mean you've been hanging around here all day on the off-chance I'd show up?'

He shrugged.

'It was a good chance, according to your mother.' He paused. 'It was the best shot I had.'

Bubbles of excitement were beginning to slip into her bloodstream. She gritted her teeth and took a sip of her strong coffee. Nothing had changed. Nothing would. He might have jetted out to see her but it was still the same Dan sitting opposite her. He probably just wanted the last word, as usual. He earned a fortune. A plane trip to the Balearics was hardly going to break the bank. She wasn't going to get sucked back into this—not now.

'It wasn't particularly easy to persuade her to help me, actually,' he added. 'Since you told her our relationship was fake.'

She looked sideways at him, one eye squinting against the sun.

'It was, Dan,' she said.

He leaned forward, his elbows on the table, and for the first time she saw how strained he looked.

'Don't say that.'

'Why did you come here?' she said. 'To make some kind of a point? To finish things between us on your terms? Go ahead and have your say, if that's what you need for closure. Get yourself the upper hand. I've got a boat to catch. I've got plans.'

She moved her hands to her sides and sat on them to maintain some distance between them.

'I know that's how I've behaved in the past.' He held his hands up. 'I hated it when you met Alistair and pulled out of our stupid agreement. I've spent years making sure *I'm* in charge in every relationship I have. I've built a life on controlling everything around me. When you just dumped the whole thing without a moment's thought I just couldn't let it slide. I manipulated the situation until it worked in my favour—agreed to bring the agreement back just so that *I* could be the one to pull out of it. I thought I'd totally nailed why it bothered me so damn much. I thought it was about calling the shots. But really I think you've always meant more to me than I realised.'

He paused, held her gaze.

'I didn't track you down so I could make some kind of a point. I came to apologise and to try and explain.'

Her stomach was doing mad acrobatics and she moved one of her hands from underneath her legs and pressed it hard.

'Go on,' she said.

'I told you how things were with Maggie,' he said. 'The thing is, it wasn't just a break-up with Maggie— something that's tough but that you reconcile in time. There was this underlying feeling I've never been able to shake—that there was my one chance and I lost it. I never had that sense of belonging when I was growing up, and when Maggie got pregnant it felt like a gift. It was my opportunity to have a family and I would have done whatever it took to protect that.'

He sighed.

'Of course what it really boiled down to was an idea. I had this whole idealistic future mapped out in my head. Birthdays, holidays, where we were going to live. My family was going to want for nothing. I think Maggie understood the two of us better. If I'm honest, when she walked away, I think losing that whole dream future I'd been cultivating hurt a hell of a lot more than losing Maggie. I knew it, too, you see. It wasn't really working between us. If she hadn't got pregnant we might have carried on seeing each other for a few more months, then we would have gone our separate ways—wherever our work ambitions led us. We were fun. We were no-strings. It was never meant to be anything serious. Her pregnancy changed all of that. A baby on the way is one hell of a big string attached. Maggie didn't want me to look out for her. After we lost the baby it became very clear that for her any future we had together was gone. There was no alternative future—not for Maggie. She found it easier to cut all ties than to stick it out with me. And I knew that she was right. Because family hasn't exactly been my finest hour, has it?'

She held his gaze. She couldn't stop her hand this time as she reached across the table and touched his arm lightly.

'None of that means you're some kind of failure. It just means you haven't given yourself a proper chance.'

'I had absolutely no desire to give family a proper chance. Not when it ended up like that. It just seemed easier to accept that I'm not a family guy. And there were compensations.'

He gave her a wry smile. She smiled back.

'You mean your little black book of girlies?'

'I thought if I was going to cut myself off from family

life I might as well make the most of what the bachelor lifestyle has to offer. Don't get the idea that I've wallowed in misery for the last ten years or so, because I haven't. I've had a brilliant time. It's only very recently that…' He trailed off.

'What?'

He looked at her then and the look in his eyes made her heart flip over.

'That it began to feel…I don't know…hollow. Nothing seemed to give me the buzz that it used to. I kept trying to up the stakes—pitching for tougher contracts, brainstorming new business ideas. Dating just lost its appeal. I felt like I was doing the rounds—the same old thing, the same old conversations. I couldn't work out what it was I needed to fix that. And then you met Alistair.'

She glanced along the harbourside. The queue for her boat trip was gradually diminishing as people stepped into the boat. She should wrap this up…crack on with her plans.

But hearing him out suddenly felt like the most important thing in the world. She told herself it didn't mean her resolve was weakening, and for Pete's sake there were other boat trips.

'I don't think I'd considered you in that way before. I hadn't let myself. I'd conditioned myself to centre everything in my life on work. But suddenly you had all these big plans—you were buzzing with happiness, you were taking a risk—and I was stuck there on the same old treadmill. I didn't like it. I think I was fed up with my own life. But it's been so long. I've really typecast myself as bachelor playboy. I thought that was who I am. I didn't think I could be anyone else.'

She covered his hand with hers and squeezed it.

A sympathy squeeze. Not a leaping-into-your-arms-is-imminent squeeze. The hope that had begun to grow in his heart when she hadn't simply left the table at the get-go faltered.

'Alistair did me a favour,' she said. 'Until I met him I think I could quite easily have carried on in that same old rut I was in, pretty much indefinitely. Thinking one day you might come to your senses and show some interest in me—'

'Emma…' he cut in urgently.

She shook her head and held up a hand to stop him.

'The crazy thing about that was that I *knew* exactly what you were like. I'd seen it first-hand for months. Different women, same old short-term thing… You never changed for any of them. I used to think they were mad—couldn't they *see* what you were like? Didn't they *know* it was a recipe for disaster, getting involved with you? And then I went right ahead and did exactly the same thing.'

'It wasn't the same. You and I are different. *I'm* different.'

She was shaking her head.

'We don't want the same things, Dan. We're fundamentally mismatched. If I've managed to salvage one thing from the stupid mess with Alistair it's that I know I want to be with someone who puts our relationship first, above anything else. Above some stupid dream of a film career.' She paused. 'Above a crazy work ethic.'

'I want us to be together.'

'Back at the wedding…what you said about me and Adam…' She looked down at her fingers. 'You told me I *liked* living in Adam's shadow. That I was wallowing in always being the one who didn't measure up. And you were right. Knowing I'd be perceived as a failure was the perfect excuse for not trying things, for staying safe. All this time—right back since school, where it felt like nothing I did was right—I've been living in Adam's shadow, and somewhere along the way I learned to prefer it. It made everything easier. Doomed not to measure up, so why bother trying?'

'But you've done brilliantly at work. You're sought after. You do a great job.'

She shook her head, a rueful smile touching her lips.

'The one area I knew I could succeed at, yes. That was a safe bet, too. I made sure I picked a job that doesn't depend on other people's perception of you for success. And something as far removed from Adam's work as possible. I don't even think it was a conscious decision— it was more of an instinctive self-preservation thing that I've been cultivating since I was a stupid, oversensitive teenager.'

She looked up at him then and the look in her eyes wrenched at his heart.

'I even deluded myself, Dan,' she said. 'I thought the single most essential thing, if I was to find someone, was for them to put me first for once. That was my bloody dating criteria, for Pete's sake! Being important to someone. Anyone.'

She threw a hand up.

'Alistair would've done. An idiot like him! If he'd carried on treating me like a princess I'd probably still be there with him, feeling smug and telling myself I was happy with that self-centred moron. I was missing the point completely. The person I really want to be important to is myself. *I* never thought I was worthwhile, but it was easier to put that on other people. I thought I could get self-esteem by keeping away from my parents, moving to London, fobbing them off with a fake life of the sort I thought I should have. But all along that was part of the problem. I liked my fake life better than my real one, too. I never really wanted to be me.'

'I want you to be you,' he said. 'There's not one single thing I'd change about you. Not even your obsessive overpacking for one weekend, which fills me with horror at what you might be like to actually *live* with—how much *stuff* you might bring into my life. I've never wanted anything more. I was scared. Too scared to give our relationship everything I've got because I didn't want to risk losing it. My track record sucks. I couldn't afford to buy into it completely because I couldn't bear to lose you.'

He reached a hand out and tucked a stray lock of her hair behind her ear. She reached for his hand, caught it and held it against her face. But her eyes were tortured, as if she were determined to stick to her decision regardless of how much it hurt.

'What about kids?' she said quietly, and his heart turned over softly. 'What about your glass furniture and your bachelor pad and your determination never to have a family of your own? Because that stuff *matters,* Dan. I'm only just starting to find myself here, but what if I want to have kids in the future? Are you going to run for the horizon?'

A smile touched his lips at that, but her face was deadly serious. Inside his spirits soared.

'I never thought I'd have another chance at family,' he said. 'I know I've built a life that reflects that, but it's all window dressing—all peripheral stuff that I've built up to convince myself as much as anyone else that I'm living the bachelor dream. Truth is, the bachelor dream is pretty bloody lonely. I want to be with you—whatever that involves.'

The thought of a future with her by his side, the possibility of a family of his own with her, filled him with such bittersweet happiness that his throat constricted and he blinked hard and tried to swallow it away.

'So what are you suggesting?' she said, her eyes narrowing. 'Another crack at the plus-one agreement, just with a few more terms and conditions? Maybe with me living in?'

He shook his head, looked into her eyes in the hope that he could convince her.

'The agreement is dissolved,' he said. 'It's over—just like it should have been after that weekend. Months before that, even. I was just looking for a way to keep seeing you that held something back.' He paused. 'But by doing that I've undervalued you. I didn't know until I lost you that I'd taken that risk already. Trying to keep some distance couldn't change that. I love you, Emma. I'm *in* love with you.'

Silence as she looked into his eyes, except for the faint sound as she caught her breath. The guarded expression didn't lift.

'That's all very well, but you've got your business to think of. I'm going travelling. I'm doing something for *me* for a change. I want my life to go in a different direction. I don't want to end up some bitter, twisted woman trying to live my kids' lives for them because I've done such a crap job at living my own life that I'm totally dissatisfied with it. You can't just expect me to throw in the towel on all my plans because you've decided you want to give our relationship a proper go. Not after everything that's happened.'

'I don't expect you to back out of all your plans. I'll come with you.'

She laughed out loud at that and he realised just how entrenched his work ethic had seemed to the outside world.

She shook her head. 'That's never going to work and we both know it. What would happen to your business? You can't even leave it alone for a weekend without carting your laptop and your damn mobile office with you. You're the biggest work control freak in the universe.'

She stood up then and his heart dropped through his chest.

'I'll do delegation for you!' he blurted.

'You'll what?'

She looked back at him, her nose wrinkled, amusement lifting the corner of her mouth.

'I'll delegate. For you, I'll delegate. Give me a few weeks to promote someone to manager and do a handover and then I'll fly out and join you. Doesn't matter where you are—you choose the itinerary. We'll have a sabbatical together.'

A moment passed during which he was convinced he'd lost her, that there was nothing he could do or say that would persuade her.

He stood up next to her, took her hand in his, tugged her back down onto the seat beside him. The fact that she went willingly he took as a positive sign. At least she wasn't running for the boat without hearing him out.

'Please, Emma,' he said. 'I know how it sounds. I know I haven't got a great track record when it comes to taking time off work. But this is different. This isn't just some holiday. This is *you*. You're more important to me than the business. You're more important to me than anything.'

She looked down at his hand in hers, tentative happiness spreading slowly through her. He was ready to put her first. And she knew how much that must cost him after what had happened to him in the past. He'd spent the last decade not letting anyone or anything become important to him.

She laced her fingers through his, finally letting herself believe, and offered him a smile and a nod.

'You realise that if you take me, you take my family, too?' she said, and then he was kneeling in front of her.

'Your mother can organise the wedding,' he said, taking both her hands in his.

* * * * *

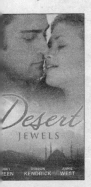 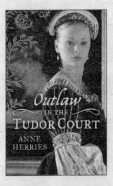 

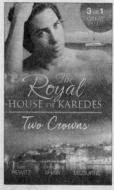

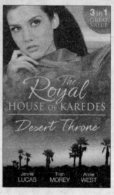

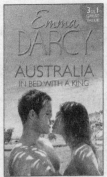
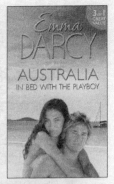

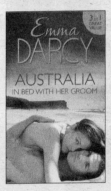